跟**老外**聊天
有**這本就夠了**

本書讓你隨意翻開就會說
盡情跟老外哈拉！

用一句簡單的英文，
跨出溝通交流的第一步！

國家圖書館出版品預行編目資料

跟老外聊天有這本就夠了 / 何維綺著

-- 二版. -- 新北市：雅典文化，民109.08

面；　公分. --（全民學英文；57）

ISBN 978-986-98710-7-5(平裝附光碟片)

1. 英語　　2. 句法

805.169　　　　　　　　　　　　　109008151

全民學英文系列 57

跟老外聊天有這本就夠了

著／何維綺
責任編輯／張文娟
美術編輯／鄭孝儀
封面設計／宋昀儒

法律顧問：方圓法律事務所／涂成樞律師

總經銷：永續圖書有限公司

永續圖書線上購物網
www.foreverbooks.com.tw

出版日／2020年08月

雅典文化

出版社

22103　新北市汐止區大同路三段194號9樓之1

TEL　（02）8647-3663

FAX　（02）8647-3660

序言
跟老外聊天有這本就夠了

　　台灣今日已處於一個高度國際化的環境，舉凡教育、工作、企業、政治、文化等，各種生活中的環節皆與世界各國緊緊相扣。生活中的各種場合，不論是教室、會議、商業交涉、文化會展等等，需要與國際人士用英文溝通或是交流的機率也相當高，全球化的趨勢在全世界蔓延，而「英文語言力」在目前全球化的時代中，更顯重要。

　　「英文語言力」當然包括了聽、說、讀、寫四個主要部分，但對許多出社會的人或是想跟外國人交朋友的人來說，面對面與國際人士接觸時，第一眼要「破冰」就非常困難，好像怎麼樣都說不出來那一句簡單的英文來跨出溝通交流的第一步，滿肚子的善意和想法只能藏在肚子裡，臉上

掛著傻笑，聊天有如登上喜馬拉雅山般的難事。

　　「有那麼難嗎？」本書特別根據與老外碰面的三個主要的不同情境：「工作場合、學習場合、朋友場合」，捨棄長串的英文，彙整各種情境常用的短句，讓你隨意翻開就會說，可以盡情地哈拉！讀過本書，你將明白只要學會了不同場合中的基本用語，反覆跟著本書附贈的mp3練習，就可輕易地「破冰」，進一步與外國人交談，拉近彼此的距離，讓你在面對外國人時，能明確的表達出自己的意思，很快就能夠跟老外混熟，進一步在「工作上、學習上、友誼上」，都能更有自信去達到想要的境界。

Chapter 1
工作場合
(In the Workplace)

目
錄

Chapter 2
學習場合
(On Learning Occasions)

Chapter 3
朋友場合
(Being with Friends)

目
錄

目
錄

Chapter

工作場合
(In the Workplace)

Lesson1
去機場接客戶
(Picking up Customers at the Airport)

在今日國際化的環境裡,職場上被派予赴機場迎接客戶的機會越來越常見,與其擔心沒有足夠的英文能力去面對,不如先一步熟悉機場各種情境,做好事先的演練,讓國外的客戶留下好印象,並增高事業合作成功的可能性。

此部分的內容主要為客戶出關後迎接時的用語,以及向客戶說明行程的安排、交通工具的安排以及乘坐時的寒暄用語。

①工作場合

②學習場合

③朋友場合

引言的關鍵單字或片語:

1. airport [`ɛr͵port]   (名詞)機場

2. greet [grit]   (動詞)迎接

3. client [`klaɪənt]   (名詞)客戶

4. immigration [͵ɪmə`greʃən]
   (名詞)入境審查

5. schedule [`skɛdʒʊl]   (名詞)行程表,
   計劃表

6. traffic arrangements [`træfɪk] [ə`rendʒmənts]
   (名詞片語)交通安排

1. 出關後碰面
(meeting after immigration)

相關用語

1. You must be Kelly.
   您一定就是凱莉吧。

2. Nice to meet you, Mr. Ho.
   很高興見到你，何先生。

3. Welcome to Taiwan!
   歡迎來到台灣！

4. My name is Vicky.
   我是維琪。

5. How was your flight?
   您旅途還順利嗎？

6. Allow me to take your suitcase.
   讓我來替您拿行李箱。

7. Let me give you the hotel information.
   讓我把飯店訊息給您。

單字、片語、句型解說

●1. meet [mit]

▶ (動詞) 遇見 【三態：meet/met/met】

例 I met her at the station.
我在車站遇見她。

●2. flight [flaɪt]

▶ (名詞) 飛行，航程

例 It's a long flight.
這是趟長途飛行。

●3. allow [əˋlaʊ]

▶ (動詞) 允許 【三態：allow/allowed/allowed】

例 He allowed us to smoke.
他允許我們抽煙。

●4. suitcase [ˋsutˌkes]

▶ (名詞) 行李箱

例 I need a suitcase.
我需要一個行李箱。

❶ 工作場合

❷ 學習場合

❸ 朋友場合

●5. let [lɛt]

▶ (動詞) 讓，允許　　　　　　　　　　**MP3** 003

例 Let me do it.
讓我來吧。

●6. give [gɪv]

▶ (動詞) 給【三態：give/gave/given】

例 Please give me a glass of water.
請給我一杯水。

●7. information [ˌɪnfəˈmeʃən]

▶ (名詞) 資訊

例 Can you give me some information
about the hotel?
你可以給我一些飯店的相關訊息嗎？

【補充】information desk [ˌɪnfəˈmeʃən] [dɛsk]

(名詞片語) 服務台

例 Excuse me, do you know where the
information desk is?
不好意思，您知道服務台在哪裡嗎？

2. 行程說明
(schedule arrangement)

相關用語

1. We are getting to the hotel first.
   我們會先去飯店。

2. We will be dropping you off at the hotel.
   我們會放您在飯店下車。

3. We can stop somewhere on the way.
   我們可以在路上稍作停留。

4. Do you need to exchange some money?
   你需要換錢嗎？

5. The meeting will be held at 9:00 a.m. tomorrow.
   會議在明早九點召開。

6. We will pick you up at 8:30 a.m. tomorrow.
   我們明早八點半會來接你。

① 工作場合
② 學習場合
③ 朋友場合

7. We will have lunch at a restaurant near the company tomorrow.

明天我們會在公司附近的一家餐廳用中餐。

 004

單字、片語、句型解說

●1. drop off [drɑp] [ɔf]

▶ (動詞片語) 中途卸客

例 Drop her off at the hotel.
在飯店讓她下車。

●2. stop [stɑp]

▶ (動詞) 停止 【三態：stop/stopped/stopped】

例 Stop talking to me.
不要再對我說話了。

●3. somewhere [`sʌmˌhwɛr]

▶ (副詞) 某處

例 Let's go out somewhere.
我們到什麼地方玩玩吧。

•4. on the way [ɑn] [ðə] [we]

▸ (介係詞片語) 途中

例 We are on the way to school.
我們在去學校的路上。

•5. exchange [ɪksˋtʃendʒ]

▸ (動詞) 交換

【三態：exchange/exchanged/exchanged】

例 He needs to exchange some money.
他需要換些錢。

•6. meeting [ˋmitɪŋ]

▸ 會議

例 I am at a meeting.
我在開會。

•7. hold [hold]

▸ (動詞) 舉行 【三態：hold/held/held】

例 They will hold a meeting tomorrow.
他們明天將開會。

•8. pick up [pɪk] [ʌp]

▸ (動詞片語) 接…人

例 Mary will pick me up at the hotel.
瑪麗會來飯店接我。

❶ 工作場合

❷ 學習場合

❸ 朋友場合

●9. restaurant [ˋrɛstərənt]

▶ (名詞) 餐廳

例 I had dinner at a French restaurant yesterday.
昨天我在一家法式餐廳用晚餐。

●10. near [nɪr]

▶ (介係詞) 在…附近

例 I live near a school.
我住在學校附近。

▶▶▶▶ 3. 交通安排
(transport arrangements)

相關用語

1. How are we getting to the hotel?
   我們怎麼去飯店？

2. This way. We have a car.
   往這邊走。我們有備車。

3. Please follow me. We are going to take a bus.
   請跟我來。我們將搭遊覽車。

4. There is a BMW waiting for us.
   寶馬汽車正等著我們。

5. We will be taking a taxi.
   我們將搭計程車。

6. I will call you a cab.
   我會幫您叫計程車。

7. Do you need to pick up something on the way to the hotel?
   在前往飯店的路上，你需要買些東西嗎？

❶ 工作場合

❷ 學習場合

❸ 朋友場合

單字、片語、句型解說

●1. get to [gɛt] [tu]+地方

▶ (動詞片語) 到達…地方

例 We are getting to the station.
我們將前往車站。

●2. follow [`falo]

▶ (動詞) 跟隨 【follow/followed/followed】

例 Please follow me to the meeting room.
請跟著我到會議室。

●3. wait for [wet] [fɔr]+人

▶ (動詞片語)等待…人

例 Please wait for me.
請等我。

●4. call [kɔl]

▶ (動詞) 呼喚、召喚 【三態：call/called/called】

例 Can you call me a taxi?
你可以幫我叫計程車嗎？

●5. cab [kæb]

▶ (名詞) 計程車

例 Please call a cab for me.
請幫我叫計程車。

4. 搭乘交通工具時
(in the vehicles)

相關用語

1. Are you hungry?
   您餓了嗎？

2. I am starving.
   我現在肚子好餓。

3. We can stop at a restaurant, if you're hungry.
   如果您餓了的話，我們可以找家餐廳稍作停留。

4. Are you interested in Chinese food?
   您對中國菜感興趣嗎？

5. This is my cell phone number.
   這是我的手機號碼。

6. Call me if anything comes up.
   萬一有什麼事，打電話給我。

7. You need to get a good rest.
   您需要好好休息一下。

單字、片語、句型解說

● 1. hungry [ˋhʌŋgrɪ]

▶ (形容詞) 飢餓的

例 I am so hungry!
我肚子好餓喔！

● 2. starving [ˋstɑrvɪŋ]

▶ (形容詞) 飢餓的

例 He is starving to death.
他快餓死了。

● 3. interested [ˋɪntərɪstɪd]

▶ (形容詞) 感到興趣的

例 I am interested in English.
我對英文感興趣。

● 4. come up [kʌm] [ʌp]

▶ (動詞片語) 發生

例 Let me know if anything comes up.
如果有什麼事，要讓我知道。

● 5. need [nid]

▶ (動詞) 需要 【三態：need/needed/needed】

例 I need your help.
我需要你的幫助。

Lesson 2

抵達住宿地時
(Upon Arriving at the Accommodations)

通常在接機後,為了讓客戶能有充分的休息,以便養足精神開啟日後的公務行程,事先安排好住宿,並使之安頓下來是必要的接待禮儀。

一般而言,公務上的客戶以安排在飯店住宿居多。為了讓客戶早點安頓下來,幫助辦理入住登記手續、告知飯店提供的服務,以及預約隔日的行程是必要的步驟。另外,最好也提供客戶聯絡的方式,除了讓客戶安心,也可以在緊急時提供協助。

① 工作場合

② 學習場合

③ 朋友場合

引言的關鍵單字或片語:

1. accommodation [əˌkɑmə`deʃən]
   (名詞)住宿

2. hotel [ho`tɛl]　　　(名詞)飯店

3. check in [tʃɛk] [ɪn]　(動詞片語)
   到達並登記

4. hotel services [ho`tɛl] [`sɝvɪsɪz]
   (名詞片語)飯店服務

5. contact information [`kɑntækt] [ˌɪnfə`meʃən]
   (名詞片語)聯絡方式

6. assistance [ə`sɪstəns]　(名詞)協助

►►►►► **1.** 環境說明
(environment description)

相關用語

1. This is a 5-star hotel.
   這是一家五星級飯店。

2. This hotel offers outstanding service.
   這家飯店的服務非常好。

3. You can have a room with a double bed.
   您可以住雙人床的房間。

4. Please follow me to your room.
   請跟著我到您的房間。

5. They speak good English at this hotel.
   這家飯店的服務人員英文講得很流利。

6. You can relax at the coffee shop and bar at this hotel.
   您可以在這家飯店的咖啡廳和酒吧裡調劑一下身心。

7. There is a free breakfast from seven to ten in the morning.
   早上七點到十點供有免費的早餐。

單字、片語、句型解說

●1. offer [`ɔfə]

▶ (動詞) 提供 【三態：offer/offered/offered】

例 She offered me a cup of tea.
她端給我一杯茶。

●2. outstanding [`aʊt`stændɪŋ]

▶ (形容詞) 傑出的

例 He is an outstanding teacher.
他是一位很棒的老師。

●3. service [`sɜvɪs]

▶ (名詞) 服務

例 That hotel is famous for its service.
那家飯店以其服務而聞名。

●4. double [`dʌbl]

▶ (形容詞) 雙人的

例 I want to reserve a double room.
我想要訂一間雙人房。

●5. follow [`falo]

▶ (動詞) 跟隨 【三態：follow/followed/followed】

例 Please follow me.
請跟我來。

●6. speak [spik]

▶ (動詞) 說 【三態：speak/spoke/spoken】

例 Can you speak English?
你會說英文嗎？

●7. relax [rɪ`læks]

▶ (動詞) 放鬆 【三態：relax/relaxed/relaxed】

例 He took a glass of beer to relax.
他喝杯啤酒輕鬆一下。

●8. bar [bɑr]

▶ (名詞) 酒吧

例 There are two bars in this hotel.
這家飯店有兩間酒吧。

●9. free [fri]

▶ (形容詞) 免費的

例 Tea is free at this restaurant.
這家餐廳的茶是免費的。

●10. breakfast [`brɛkfəst]

▶ (名詞) 早餐

例 This hotel serves free breakfasts.
這家飯店供應免費的早餐。

2. 辦理入住登記手續 (check in)

相關用語

1. My company made a reservation for me.
   我的公司替我訂了房間。

2. Let me check that for you, sir.
   讓我替您查一查(是否已訂房)。

3. Your room is ready. Your room number is 201.
   您的房間已備好。您的房間號碼是二〇一。

4. Here's your room key.
   這是您房間的鑰匙。

5. You're all checked in.
   您的入住手續都辦理好了。

6. Let's bring your bags upstairs.
   我們將行李拿上樓吧。

7. Do you need a wake-up call?
   需要打電話叫您起床嗎？

❶ 工作場合

❷ 學習場合

❸ 朋友場合

MP3 010

單字、片語、句型解說

● 1. reservation [ˌrɛzɚˈveʃən]

(名詞) 預約

例 I need to make reservations for two rooms at the hotel.
我需要在這個旅館預訂兩個房間。

● 2. check [tʃɛk]

(動詞) 檢查 【三態：check/checked/checked】

例 Check to see if he has made a reservation.
查一下他是否有預約。

● 3. ready [ˈrɛdɪ]

(形容詞) 準備好的

例 Are you ready to go?
你準備好要走了嗎？

● 4. number [ˈnʌmbɚ]

(名詞) 號碼

例 What is your room number?
你住幾號房？

●5. check in [tʃɛk] [ɪn]

► (動詞片語) 到達並登記

例 You need to check in first.
你必須先辦理入住登記手續。

●6. bring [brɪŋ]

► (動詞) 帶來　【bring/brought/brought】

例 Don't forget to bring your book.
別忘記帶書來。

●7. upstairs [ˋʌpˋstɛrz]

► (副詞) 上樓

例 He is running upstairs.
他正往樓上跑去。

●8. a wake-up call [ə] [ˋwekˏʌp] [kɔl]

► (名詞片語) 電話叫醒服務

例 I can give you a wake-up call.
我可以打電話叫您起床。

3. 飯店服務
(hotel services information)

相關用語

1. If you need any help, you can call us.
   如需任何服務，請來電。

2. Do you need a morning call tomorrow morning?
   明天早上需要飯店打電話叫您起床嗎？

3. This brochure is about the sightseeing.
   這手冊備有觀光資訊。

4. This hotel serves free coffee and tea throughout the day.
   這家飯店全天供應免費的咖啡跟茶。

5. This hotel offers laundry service.
   這家飯店提供洗衣服務。

6. This hotel also offers parking and taxi dispatch services.
   這家飯店也提供停車及叫車的服務。

7. There is a mini-bar in your hotel room.
   在您的飯店房間裡面有一個迷你酒吧。

單字、片語、句型解說

●1. help [hɛlp]

▶ (名詞) 幫助

例 Do you need any help?
我可以幫你嗎？

●2. call [kɔl]

▶ (動詞) 打電話 【三態：call/called/called】

例 Please call me this afternoon.
今天下午請打個電話給我。

●3. brochure [bro`ʃʊr]

▶ (名詞) 小冊子

例 This is a brochure on vacations.
這是本度假手冊。

●4. sightseeing [`saɪtˌsiɪŋ]

▶ (名詞) 觀光

例 I'd like to do some sightseeing.
我想去觀光。

●5. serve [sɝv]

▶ (動詞) 供應 【三態：serve/served/served】

例 Does the restaurant serve free tea?
餐廳有供應免費的茶嗎？

MP3 012

●6. free [fri]

▶ (形容詞) 免費的

例 Coffee is free today.
今天咖啡免費供應。

●7. throughout [θru`aʊt]

▶ (介係詞) 貫穿，從頭到尾

例 He slept throughtout the day.
他睡了一整天。

●8. laundry [`lɔndrɪ]

▶ (名詞) 洗衣店

例 Please send it to the laundry.
請把它送到洗衣店去。

●9. parking [`parkɪŋ]

▶ (名詞) 停車

例 There is no parking space.
沒有停車位。

●10. dispatch [dɪ`spætʃ]

▶ (名詞) 派遣

例 Do you need taxi dispatch services?
您需要叫計程車嗎？

4. 明日行程
(tomorrow's visit arrangements)

相關用語

1. We should get to the company at 10:00 a.m.
   我們要在早上十點到公司。

2. The meeting will start at 10:30 a.m.
   會議將在早上十點半召開。

3. We will pick you up around 9:30 a.m.
   我們在早上九點半左右會來接你。

4. There are a few people I'd like you to meet.
   我想讓您見一些人。

5. We will show you around.
   我們會帶您到處參觀。

6. We will have dinner at a famous Chinese restaurant in Taipei.
   我們會在台北一家有名的中式餐廳用晚餐。

7. I'll pay for dinner tomorrow.
   明天晚餐我請客。

❶ 工作場合

❷ 學習場合

❸ 朋友場合

MP3 013

單字、片語、句型解說

●1. should [ʃʊd]

→ (助動詞) 應該

例 I should work hard.
我應該要努力工作。

●2. start [stɑrt]

→ (動詞) 開始 【start/started/started】

例 When will the meeting start?
會議幾點開始？

●3. around [əˋraʊnd]

→ (介係詞) 大約

例 She went to Taipei around 2010.
她約莫在二〇一〇年去到台北。

●4. there + be 動詞+名詞(片語)…

→ 【有…】

例 There are many people in the park.
公園裡有很多人。

●5. a few [ə] [fju]

→ (形容詞片語) 一些

例 There are a few students in the classroom.
教室裡有一些學生。

●6. would like [wʊd] [laɪk]+人 +to V

▶ 【想要某人去…】

例 I would like you to talk to her.
我希望你跟她說話。

●7. show [ʃo]+人+around [əˋraʊnd]

▶ (動詞片語) 帶…人到處參觀

例 I'll show you around.
我會帶你到處看看。

●8. have +三餐(breakfast/lunch/dinner)

▶ 【用…餐】

例 I hope to have dinner with you tonight.
今晚我希望與你共進晚餐。

●9. famous [ˋfeməs]

▶ (形容詞) 著名的

例 He is a famous singer.
他是位著名的歌星。

●10. pay [pe]

▶ (動詞) 付 【三態：pay/paid/paid】

例 You don't need to pay me anything.
你不需要付給我任何報酬。

🎧 014

5. 聯絡方式
(contact information)

相關用語

1. This is my business card.
   這是我的名片。

2. Do you have my cell phone number?
   您有我的手機號碼嗎？

3. Please call me at this number : (02)
   86473663.
   請撥打這個電話號碼(02)86473663與我聯繫。

4. The phone number of our company is
   : (02) 86473663.
   我們公司的電話是(02)86473663。

5. You can also contact us by e-mail:
   yungjiuh@ms45.hinet.net.
   您也可以透過電子郵件與我們聯繫，地址為
   yungjiuh@ms45.hinet.net.

6. This is my company address.
   這是我公司地址。

單字、片語、句型解說

●1. business card [ˋbɪznɪs] [kɑrd]

▶ (名詞片語) 名片

例 Do you have a business card?
您有名片嗎？

●2. cell phone[ˋsɛlfon]

▶ (名詞片語) 手機

例 Using a cell phone is convenient.
使用手機很方便。

●3. number [ˋnʌmbɚ]

▶ (名詞) 號碼

例 Seven is my lucky number.
七是我的幸運號碼。

●4. contact [ˋkɑntækt]

▶ (動詞) 聯繫

【三態：contact/contacted/contacted】

例 I will contact you by telephone.
我將打電話與您聯繫。

●5. address[əˋdrɛs]

▶ (名詞) 地址

例 Please tell me your home address.
請告訴我你家的地址。

❶ 工作場合
❷ 學習場合
❸ 朋友場合

🎵 **015**

Lesson3
抵達會議現場時
(Upon Arriving at the Conference Site)

　　客戶在飯店休息過後，通常在接下來的幾天，會有一連串的商務參訪行程，為了讓來自國外的客戶感受到禮遇及重視，負責接待的職員最好要先了解客戶方的參訪行程，並對行程所到之地的環境做說明，並於參訪現場視客戶需要隨時提供方向指引，以及於參訪會議開始前做簡短的會議流程說明。通常在會議結束後，主辦單位會招待與會者午餐或晚餐，此時更是與客戶輕鬆談論飲食文化的好時機，趁機拉近彼此間的距離。

　　而不論是在抵達會議場合之初、參與會議的過程、以及用餐的時間，都很有可能遇到很多的貴賓，因此也必須熟悉介紹的相關用語，達到好的人際互動，讓整個行程在活動結束歡送後畫下美好的句點。

引言的關鍵單字或片語：

1. a business visit [ə] [ˋbɪznɪs] [ˋvɪzɪt]
   (名詞片語)商務參訪

2. environment description [ɪnˋvaɪrənmənt]
   [dɪˋskrɪpʃən] (名詞片語)環境說明，環境敘述

3. give directions [gɪv] [dəˋrɛkʃənz]
   (動詞片語)指引方向

4. agenda [əˋdʒɛndə]　　(名詞)議程

5. food culture [fud] [ˋkʌltʃɚ]
   (名詞片語)飲食文化

6. guest [gɛst]　　(名詞)客人，賓客

7. introduction [͵ɪntrəˋdʌkʃən]
   (名詞)介紹

8. interpersonal interaction [͵ɪntɚˋpɝsən!]
   [͵ɪntɚˋækʃən]　　(名詞片語)人際互動

9. farewell [ˋfɛrˋwɛl]　　(名詞)告別，再見

10. a good evening [ə] [gʊd] [ˋivnɪŋ]
    (名詞片語)美好的夜晚

❶ 工作場合

❷ 學習場合

❸ 朋友場合

1. 環境說明
(environment description)

相關用語

1. The conference is held at our company.
   會議在我們的公司舉行。

2. There will be a business show also on the second floor.
   二樓也會有商展。

3. We could also take a look at the factory.
   我們也可以看一下廠房。

4. It's also possible to have a tour of the company facilities.
   要參觀公司的設施也是可以的。

5. You can find a toilet on every floor.
   在每層樓你都可以找到廁所。

6. Free tea and coffee are available on the table.
   桌上供有免費的茶及咖啡。

單字、片語、句型解說

●1. conference [ˈkɑnfərəns]

▶ (名詞) 會議

例 The conference is about education.
這是個有關教育的會議。

●2. business show [ˈbɪznɪs] [ʃo]

▶ (名詞片語) 商展

例 The business show will last for three days.
商展將持續三天。

●3. floor [flor]

▶ (名詞) 樓層

例 He lives on the second floor.
他住在二樓。

●4. factory [ˈfæktərɪ]

▶ (名詞) 工廠

例 He is a factory worker.
他是工廠工人。

●5. possible [ˈpɑsəb!]

▶ (形容詞) 可能的

例 Is it possible for you to come here?
你有可能來這裡嗎？

●6. tour [tʊr]

▶ (名詞) 遊覽

例 Kelly hopes to make a tour around Japan.
凱莉希望到日本旅行。

●7. facility [fə`sɪlətɪ]

▶ (名詞) 設施、設備 【複數 facilities】

例 I have no cooking facilities in my house.
我家沒有煮飯做菜的設備。

●8. available [ə`veləb!]

▶ (形容詞) 可得的

例 The book is not available now.
這本書現在買不到。

相關用語

1. Go up to the third floor, and you'll find the toilet on your right.
   上三樓，廁所就在右手邊。

2. Go straight until you get to the conference room.
   直走到會議室。

3. The factory is across the street.
   廠房在對街的那一邊。

4. The restaurant is on your left, next to the factory.
   餐廳在左手邊，緊鄰廠房。

5. The business show is only about 5 minutes from here.
   商展離這裡約五分鐘路程。

6. There is a factory at the corner.
   廠房在轉角處。

7. Over here on the left, you can see the office.

在左手邊這兒，您可以看到辦公室。

單字、片語、句型解說

●1. right [raɪt]

▶ (名詞) 右邊

例 He is standing on her right.
他正站在她右邊。

●2. straight [stret]

▶ (副詞) 直地

例 Go straight down the road.
沿著這條路一直走。

●3. until [ən`tɪl]

▶ (副詞連接詞) 直到

例 He lived in Taipei until his father worked in Chia-yi.
在他父親於嘉義工作前，他一直住在台北。

●4. across[ə`krɔs]

▶ (介係詞) 橫越，穿過

例 You need to walk across the street.
你需要過馬路。

●5. left [lɛft]

▶ (名詞) 左邊

例 Go straight and then turn left.
直走然後左轉。

●6. next to [`nɛkst] [tu]

▶ (介係詞片語) 緊鄰著

例 My house is next to your school.
我家在你學校旁邊。

●7. minute [`mɪnɪt]

▶ (名詞) 分鐘

例 Only five minutes are left for you.
你只剩五分鐘。

●8. corner [`kɔrnɚ]

▶ (名詞) 街角

例 I met her at a street corner.
我在街角處遇見她。

●9. over here [`ovɚ] [hɪr]

▶ （介係詞片語） 在這兒

over there [`ovɚ] [ðɛr]
（介係詞片語） 在那兒

例 There is a cat over there.
那兒有一隻貓。

▶▶▶▶ 3. 行程說明
(conference agenda)

相關用語

1. The president will give welcoming remarks at 9:00 a.m.
   總裁將於早上九點致歡迎詞。

2. There will be two keynote addresses in the morning.
   早上會有兩場主題演講。

3. You could also visit the computer exhibits on the fifth floor.
   您也可以到五樓參觀電腦用品展。

4. We will have lunch at a Chinese restaurant near the conference site.
   我們會在會議現場附近的一家中式餐廳用中餐。

5. After lunch, we will have a tour of the factory.
   中餐過後，我們會參觀廠房。

6. After the conference, a bus will take you to the hotel.
會議結束後，遊覽車會載您回飯店。

單字、片語、句型解說

●1. president [`prɛzədənt]

▶ (名詞) 總裁

例 The president will visit your company next week.
下周總裁將拜訪你們公司。

●2. welcoming remarks [`wɛlkəmɪŋ] [rɪ`marks]

▶ (名詞片語) 歡迎詞

例 Dr. Wang will give welcoming remarks before the meeting.
王博士將在會議開始前致歡迎詞。

●3. keynote address [`ki,not] [ə`drɛs]

▶ (名詞片語) 主題演講

例 The keynote address is about air pollution.
這場主題演講的內容是關於空氣汙染。

❶ 工作場合

❷ 學習場合

❸ 朋友場合

●4. visit [ˋvɪzɪt]

▶ (動詞) 參觀，拜訪

【三態：visit/visited/visited】

例 I hope to visit you next week.
我希望下周可以去看你。 **MP3 020**

●5. exhibit [ɪgˋzɪbɪt]

▶ (名詞) 展示品，展示會

例 You cannot touch the exhibits.
你不能觸摸展示品。

●6. site [saɪt]

▶ (名詞) 地點，場所

例 This school is a good site for exhibits.
這間學校是展示的好場地。

●7. after [ˋæftɚ]

▶ (介係詞) 在…之後

例 Come to my home after school.
放學後來我家。

●8. take [tek]+人+to [tu]+地方

▶ 【帶人去…地方】

例 My mother takes me to school every day.
媽媽每天帶我上學。

4. 用餐
(having a meal)

相關用語

1. Your table is in a non-smoking area.
   您的用餐位置在禁煙區。

2. Here is your menu.
   這是您的菜單。

3. The dinner hours are from 6:30 to 8:30 p.m.
   晚餐時間從六點半到八點半。

4. Vegetarian dishes are offered.
   有供應素食。

5. This restaurant serves mainly Chinese dishes.
   這家餐廳主要供應中國菜。

6. Would you like to try something different?
   你想吃點不一樣的嗎？

7. I hope you enjoy your dinner tonight.
   希望您今晚用餐愉快。

❶ 工作場合
❷ 學習場合
❸ 朋友場合

MP3 021

單字、片語、句型解說

● 1. non-smoking [ˌnɑn`smokɪŋ]

► (形容詞) 禁煙的

例 I prefer a non-smoking area.
我比較想坐在禁煙區。

● 2. area [`ɛrɪə]

► (名詞) 區域

例 There is no parking area here.
這裡沒有停車場。

● 3. menu [`mɛnju]

► (名詞) 菜單

例 Let me see what is on the menu today.
讓我看看今天菜單的內容。

● 4. vegetarian [ˌvɛdʒə`tɛrɪən]

► (形容詞) 素食的

例 My mother is looking for vegetarian recipes.
媽媽正在找素食食譜。

● 5. dish [dɪʃ]

► (名詞) 菜餚

例 Fried rice is my favorite dish.
炒飯是我最喜愛的菜餚。

● 6. offer [ˋɔfɚ]

▶ (動詞) 提供 【三態：offer/offered/offered】

例 She offered me a glass of water.
她端給我一杯水

● 7. serve [sɝv]

▶ (動詞) 供應 【三態：serve/served/served】

例 He served me a cup of tea.
他給我端上一杯茶。

● 8. mainly [ˋmenlɪ]

▶ (副詞) 主要地

例 He is mainly to blame.
主要應怪他。

● 9. would like to [wʊd] [laɪk] [tu]+V

▶ 【想要…】

例 Would you like to talk with me?
你想跟我聊聊嗎？

● 10. try [traɪ]

▶ (動詞) 嘗試 【三態：try/tried/tried】

例 I'll try to improve my English.
我會設法改善我的英文。

❶ 工作場合
❷ 學習場合
❸ 朋友場合

5. 貴賓介紹
(introduction to the guests)

相關用語

1. Let's make some introductions.
   讓我們來介紹彼此認識。

2. This is Mary.
   這位是瑪麗。

3. Nice to meet you.
   很高興見到您。

4. I'm guessing you're John.
   我猜你就是約翰吧。

5. Her name is Kelly. And I'm Vicky.
   她是凱莉，而我是維琪。

6. Let me introduce you to Mr. Ho.
   讓我向您介紹何先生。

7. Mr. Ho is the manager of the computer company.
   何先生是電腦公司的經理。

單字、片語、句型解說

●1. let's+V

▶ 【讓我們…】

例 Let's go to the movies.
我們去看電影吧。

●2. introduction [ˌɪntrəˋdʌkʃən]

▶ (名詞) 介紹

例 Please give a short introduction of
yourself.
請簡短地自我介紹。

●3. guess [gɛs]

▶ (動詞) 猜測 【三態：guess/guessed/guessed】

例 Can you guess what will happen next?
你能推測出接下來會發生什麼事嗎？

●4. let [lɛt]+人+V

▶ 【讓…人去…】

例 Please let me go.
請讓我走吧。

●5. introduce [ˌɪntrəˋdjus]

▶ (動詞) 介紹

【三態：introduce/introduced/introduced】

introduce+A+to+B 【把A介紹給B】

例 Please introduce your friends to me.
　　請介紹你的朋友給我認識。

● 6. manager [`mænɪdʒɚ]

▶ (名詞) 經理

例 Lisa is a store manager.
　　麗莎是位商店的經理。

　【補充】president [`prɛzədənt]
　（名詞）　總裁，董事長

例 William is the president of this
　　computer company.
　　威廉是這家電腦公司的董事長。

6. 結束後歡送 (saying goodbye)

相關用語

1. Well, that's it for today.
   今天的行程到這告一段落了。

2. Tomorrow morning I'll pick you up at the same time 9:00.
   明天早上一樣我會在九點來接你。

3. And we'll be visiting another company at 10:00 a.m..
   而在早上十點我們將參訪另一家公司。

4. Have a good night and I'll see you tomorrow.
   晚安,明天見。

5. I think this is where we say goodbye.
   我想這就是我們道別的地方了。

6. Hope to see you soon.
   希望很快能夠再見面。

單字、片語、句型解說

● 1. the same [ðə] [sem]

▶ (形容詞片語) 同樣的

例 I'll meet you in the same place in the classroom.
我會同樣在教室見你。

● 2. another [əˋnʌðɚ]

▶ (形容詞) 另一

例 That's another story.
那是另外一回事。

● 3. think [θɪŋk]

▶ (動詞) 想

【三態：think/thought/thought】

例 I don't think Linda will come.
我不認為琳達會來。

● 4. soon [sun]

▶ (副詞) 不久地

例 It will soon be winter.
很快就要冬天了。

Lesson4
招待客戶
(Entertaining the Clients)

　　來自遠方的客戶，歷經了一連串的商務行程之後，難免希望可以利用私下的時間多認識台灣，舉凡台灣的美食、美景、名產等，都是他們會想嘗試及體驗的道地特色。另外，商場上的互動也常涉及與客戶外出應酬，有時難免也要飲酒作樂一番，如果遇上喜歡高歌一曲的客戶，此時投其所好帶他去唱卡拉OK，這樣一來，極有可能客戶不再只是生意上的伙伴，而會變成麻吉的朋友了！你不但能贏得生意，也將贏得友誼，所以瞭解如何應付這些狀況的英文用語，就提高了你可以雙贏的局面。

❶ 工作場合

❷ 學習場合

❸ 朋友場合

引言的關鍵單字或片語：

1. delicacy [ˋdɛləkəsɪ]　　(名詞)美食，佳餚

2. scenery [ˋsinərɪ]　　(名詞)風景

3. a special product [ə] [ˋspɛʃəl] [ˋprɑdəkt]
　　(名詞片語)特產

4. drinking [ˋdrɪŋkɪŋ]　　(名詞)喝酒

5. singing [`sɪŋɪŋ]　　　(名詞)唱歌

6. a business partner [ə] [`bɪznɪs] [`partnɚ]
　　　　　　　　　　(名詞片語)生意伙伴

7. friendship [`frɛndʃɪp]　(名詞)友誼

8. a win-win situation [ə] [`wɪn ˌwɪn]
[ˌsɪtʃʊ`eʃən]　　　(名詞片語)雙贏的局面

1. 介紹台灣美食
(Taiwan's delicious foods)

相關用語

1. I think you'd like to try stinky tofu.
   我想您會想嚐嚐臭豆腐。

2. What's it called?
   這個叫什麼啊？

3. It's called "oyster omelet."
   這個叫蚵仔煎。

4. It's made from oysters, eggs, and starch.
   他是由蚵仔、蛋及澱粉所製成。

5. It is often sold in night markets.
   它是夜市裡常賣的食物。

6. It tastes sour and spicy.
   嚐起來又酸又辣。

7. I think you've never had this before.
   我想你從來沒吃過這個吧。

工作場合

單字、片語、句型解說

●1. stinky tofu [`stɪŋkɪ] [`tofu]

▶ (名詞片語) 臭豆腐

例 He thinks stinky tofu is delicious.
他覺得臭豆腐美味。

●2. call [kɔl]

▶ (動詞) 稱呼，叫做【三態：call/called/called】

【這邊是被動式： be + pp = is + called】

例 Please call me Julia.
請叫我茱莉亞。

●3. oyster omelet [`ɔɪstɚ] [`ɑmlɪt]

▶ (名詞片語) 蚵仔煎

例 What's an oyster omelet made from?
蚵仔煎是由什麼做成的？

●4. 成品+be made from+材料

▶ 【成品由…所製成】

例 Beer is made from wheat.
啤酒由小麥所製成。

MP3 027

●5. starch [stɑrtʃ]

▶ (名詞) 澱粉

例 Corn contains much starch.
玉米含有大量澱粉。

●6. sell [sɛl]

▶ (動詞) 賣 【三態：sell/sold/sold】

這邊是被動式：be + pp=is + sold

例 She sold me her car.
她把車賣給我。

●7. taste [test]

▶ (動詞) 嚐起來 【三態：taste/tasted/tasted】

例 The soup tastes bitter.
這湯喝起來苦苦的。

●8. spicy [ˈspaɪsɪ]

▶ (形容詞) 辣的

例 The soup is so spicy.
這湯好辣。

●9. think [θɪŋk]

▶ (動詞) 想，認為

【三態：think/thought/thought】

例 I think you are right.
我認為你是對的。

●10. you've = you have

▶ have+had = have+pp = 現在完成式(表到目前為止的經驗)

工作場合

台灣常見美食列表(1)

美食 中文名	對照之 英文及音標	組成的 單字解說
小籠包	steamed buns [stimd] [bʌnz]	steamed (形容詞)蒸的 bun (名詞)小圓糕點
碗糕	fried white radish patty [fraɪd] [hwaɪt] [ˋrædɪʃ] [ˋpætɪ]	fried (形容詞)炸的 white(形容詞)白色的 radish (名詞)蘿蔔 patty (名詞)小餡餅
蘿蔔糕	salty rice pudding [ˋsɔltɪ][raɪs] [ˋpʊdɪŋ]	salty (形容詞)鹹的 rice (名詞)米 pudding (名詞)布丁狀物
割包	steamed sandwich [stimd] [ˋsændwɪtʃ]	steamed (形容詞)蒸的 sandwich (名詞)三明治
油條	fried bread stick [fraɪd] [brɛd] [stɪk]	fried (形容詞)炸的 bread (名詞)麵包 stick (名詞)枝條，棒

028

台灣常見美食列表(2)

美食	對照之	組成的
肉圓	Taiwanese meatball [ˌtaɪwəˈniz] [ˈmitˌbɔl]	Taiwanese (形容詞)台灣的 meatball (名詞)肉糰
筒仔米糕	rice tube pudding [raɪs] [tjub] [ˈpʊdɪŋ]	rice (名詞)米 tube (名詞)管，筒 pudding (名詞)布丁狀物
豬血糕	pigs blood cake [pɪgz] [blʌd] [kek]	pig (名詞)豬 blood (名詞)血 cake (名詞)蛋糕，糕餅
水餃	boiled dumplings [bɔɪld] [ˈdʌmplɪŋz]	boiled (形容詞)煮熟的 dumpling (名詞)餃子
珍珠奶茶	pearl milk tea [pɝl] [mɪlk] [ti]	pearl (名詞)珍珠 milk (名詞)牛奶 tea (名詞)茶

1 工作場合

台灣常見美食列表(3)

美食 中文名	對照之 英文及音標	組成的 單字解說
大腸麵線	intestine noodles [ɪnˋtɛstɪn] [ˋnud! z]	intestine (名詞)腸 noodle (名詞)麵條
蚵仔麵線	oyster thin noodles [ˋɔɪstɚ] [θɪn] [ˋnud! z]	oyster (名詞)蚵仔 thin (形容詞)細的，瘦的 noodle (名詞)麵條
米粉	rice noodles [raɪs] [ˋnud! z]	rice (名詞)米 noodle (名詞)麵條
春捲	spring rolls [sprɪŋ] [rolz]	spring (名詞)春天 roll (名詞)捲餅
潤餅	mixed vegetable roll [mɪkst] [ˋvɛdʒətəb!] [rol]	mixed (形容詞)混合的 vegetable (名詞)蔬菜 roll (名詞)捲餅

029

台灣常見美食列表(4)

美食中文名	對照之英文及音標	組成的單字解說
滷味	soy sauce flavored delicacies [sɔɪ] [sɔs] [ˋflevɚd] [ˋdɛləkəsɪz]	soy sauce (名詞片語)醬油 flavored (形容詞)調味的 delicacy (名詞)佳餚
豆干	dried tofu [draɪd] [ˋtofu]	dried (形容詞)弄乾的 tofu (名詞)豆腐
雞肉飯	turkey rice [ˋtɝkɪ] [raɪs]	turkey (名詞)火雞肉 rice (名詞)米飯
滷肉飯	braised pork rice [brezd] [pork] [raɪs]	braised (形容詞)文火燉煮的 pork (名詞)豬肉 rice (名詞)米飯
蛋炒飯	fried rice with egg [fraɪd] [raɪs] [wɪð] [ɛg]	fried (形容詞)炒的 rice (名詞)米飯 with (介係詞)有 egg (名詞)蛋

工作場合

071

▶▶▶▶▶ **2.** 餐廳特色說明
(restaurant description)

相關用語

1. This is a restaurant with a quiet atmosphere.

   這是一家氣氛寧靜的餐廳。

2. The prices at this restaurant are reasonable.

   這家餐廳價位合理。

3. You could have some local food at this restaurant.

   你在這家餐廳可以嚐到道地的食物。

4. This street is the main area for restaurants.

   餐廳多集中在這條街。

5. There are many Chinese restaurants around here.

   這附近中式餐廳林立。

6. This restaurant has piano players during dinner time.

   這家餐廳晚餐時間有鋼琴演奏。

7. Don't forget to save room for the dessert.

   別忘了留點肚子吃甜點。

 030

單字、片語、句型解說

1. quiet [ˈkwaɪət]

▶ (形容詞) 安靜的

2. atmosphere [ˈætməsˌfɪr]

▶ (名詞) 氣氛

例 I'd like a restaurant with a happy atmosphere.

我想去一家氣氛歡樂的餐廳。

3. price [praɪs]

▶ (名詞) 價格

例 What's the price of that house?

那房子要賣多少錢？

●4. reasonable [`rizənəb!]

▶ (形容詞) 合理的

例 Give me a reasonable reason.
給我一個合理的解釋。

●5. local [`lok!]

▶ (形容詞) 當地的

例 I'd like to try local food.
我想嚐嚐當地的食物。

●6. main [men]

▶ (形容詞) 主要的

例 What's the main reason for exercising?
運動主要的理由是什麼？

●7. around [ə`raʊnd]

▶ (介係詞) 在…附近

例 He likes to take a walk around the park.
他喜歡在公園附近散步。

●8. player [`pleə]

▶ (名詞) 演奏者

● 9. forget [fəˋgɛt]

▶ (動詞) 忘記

【三態：forget/forgot/forgotten】

forget+to V 【忘了去…】

例 Don't forget to call me.

別忘了打電話給我。

● 10. save [sev]

▶ (動詞) 保留 【三態：save/saved/saved】

例 Please save a room for me.

請幫我保留一個房間。

● 11. room [rum]

▶ (名詞) 空間

● 12. dessert [dɪˋzɝt]

▶ (名詞) 甜點

▶▶▶▶▶ 3. 飲酒時
(when drinking)

相關用語

1. I want a beer.
   我想喝啤酒。

2. Would you like some whiskey?
   你想喝一點威士忌嗎？

3. Cheers!
   乾杯！(= Bottoms up!)

4. Don't drink too much!
   不要喝太多啊！

5. He is getting drunk.
   他喝醉了。

6. Would you like to have more wine?
   你還要繼續喝嗎？

7. Are you ready for a refill?
   要再來一杯嗎？

單字、片語、句型解說

● 1. beer [bɪr]

▶ (名詞) 啤酒

例 Please buy me a beer, Bill.
比爾,請買罐啤酒給我。

● 2. whiskey [`hwɪskɪ]

▶ (名詞) 威士忌

例 This is the best Scotch whiskey.
這是最好的蘇格蘭威士忌。

● 3. bottom [`batəm]

▶ (名詞) 底部

例 The bottom of the car is leaking water.
這車子的底部在漏水。

● 4. drink [drɪŋk]

▶ (動詞) 喝 【三態:drink/drank/drunk】

例 This dog needs to drink some water.
這隻狗需要喝點水。

● 5. get+形容詞

▶ 【變得…】

例 It's getting warm.
天氣變暖和了。

● 6. drunk [drʌŋk]

▶ (形容詞) 喝醉酒的

例 She got drunk on nine cans of beer.
九罐啤酒下肚，她醉了。

● 7. wine [waɪn]

▶ (名詞) 酒

例 Let me help you to another glass of wine.
讓我為您再斟杯酒。

● 8. refill [ˈrifɪl]

▶ (名詞) 再裝滿

例 I want a refill, please.
請再給我一杯。

▶▶▶▶ 4. 卡拉 OK
(karaoke)

相關用語

1. Would you like to sing at a karaoke bar?

   你想去卡拉OK酒吧唱歌嗎？

2. This is the best known karaoke bar in Taipei.

   這是台北最有名的卡拉OK酒吧。

3. We would sometimes sing karaoke after work.

   下班後我們有時候會去唱歌。

4. In Taiwan, most people like to sing at Cashbox Partyworld and Holiday KTV.

   台灣大多數人喜歡去錢櫃跟好樂迪唱歌。

5. You can find your favorite songs to sing on the computer screen.

   你可以在電腦螢幕上找到最喜歡唱的歌。

6. You have such a good voice!

你的聲音真好聽！

7. We can sing for three hours.

我們可以唱三個小時。

單字、片語、句型解說

●1. known [non]

▶ (形容詞) 知名的

例 She is a known singer.

她是一個知名的歌手。

●2. sometimes [`sʌmˌtaɪmz]

▶ (副詞) 有時

例 I come to visit my teacher sometimes.

有時我會去拜訪我的老師。

●3. after work [`æftə·] [wɝk]

▶ (介係詞片語) 下班後

例 I often go shopping after work.

下班後我常去購物。

●4. most [most]

▶ (形容詞) 大多數的

例 Most people like chocolate.
大多數人喜歡巧克力。

●5. find [faɪnd]

▶ (動詞) 找到 【三態：find/found/found】

例 I can't find my wallet.
我找不到我的錢包。

●6. favorite [ˋfevərɪt]

▶ (形容詞) 最喜歡的

例 Leehom Wang is my favorite singer.
王力宏是我最喜歡的歌手。

●7. screen [skrin]

▶ (名詞) 螢幕

例 Do you know how to clean a TV screen?
你知道如何清理電視螢幕嗎？

●8. voice [vɔɪs]

▶ (名詞) 聲音，嗓子

例 She is talking in a cheerful voice.
她興高采烈地談著。

工作場合

5. 台灣景點 01
(tourist attractions in Taiwan)

相關用語

1. The Taipei Zoo is the largest city zoo in Asia.
   台北動物園是亞洲最大的都市動物園。

2. Taipei 101 is a famous landmark skyscraper in Taipei.
   台北101大樓是台北著名的地標。

3. You can enjoy various snacks in Shilin Night Market.
   在士林夜市裡你可品嚐到各種小吃。

4. The architecture of Chiang Kai-shek Memorial Hall is special and magnificent.
   中正紀念堂的建築既特別又壯麗。

5. The National Palace Museum is one of the largest art museums in the world.
   國立故宮博物院是世界上最大的藝術博物館之一。

6. Tamsui is known for beautiful sunsets and historical sites.

淡水以美麗的日落和歷史古蹟而聞名。

單字、片語、句型解說

1. large [lardʒ]

▶ (形容詞) 大的

【largest為形容詞最高級，意思為「最大的」】

例 He needs the largest box.
他需要最大的盒子。

2. Asia [ˋeʃə]

▶ (名詞) 亞洲

例 Asia is the world's largest continent.
亞洲是世界上最大的一個洲。

3. landmark [ˋlændˏmɑrk]

▶ (名詞) 地標

例 Sun-Shooting Tower is a well-known landmark in Chia-yi.
射日塔是嘉義著名的地標。

•4. skyscraper [`skaɪ,skrepɚ]

▶ (名詞) 摩天樓

例 Kaohsiung 85 Building is a famous skyscraper in Kaohsiung.
高雄85大樓是高雄著名的摩天樓。

MP3 035

•5. various [`vɛrɪəs]

▶ (形容詞) 各種各樣的

例 Eric was late for school for various reasons.
由於種種原因，艾瑞克上學遲到了。

•6. snack [snæk]

▶ (名詞) 小吃

例 She likes to eat snacks at night.
她喜歡晚上吃小吃。

•7. architecture [`ɑrkə,tɛktʃɚ]

▶ (名詞) 建築物

例 This architecture is so impressive!
這建築物真令人印象深刻！

8. special [ˈspɛʃəl]

▶ (形容詞) 特別的

例 This gift is so special!
這真是一份特別的禮物！

9. magnificent [mægˈnɪfəsənt]

▶ (形容詞) 壯麗的

例 I visited a magnificent church yesterday.
昨天我參觀了一間壯麗的教堂。

10. museum [mjuˈzɪəm]

▶ (名詞) 博物館

例 Welcome to the National Museum of History!
歡迎來到國立歷史博物館！

11. sunset [ˈsʌnˌsɛt]

▶ (名詞) 日落

例 This is a good place for watching sunsets.
這是個欣賞日落的好地方。

12. historical [hɪsˈtɔrɪk!]

▶ (形容詞) 歷史的

例 I like to see historical plays.
我喜歡看歷史劇。

5. 台灣景點 02
(tourist attractions in Taiwan)

相關用語

1. Yangmingshan National Park features many tourist sites, such as the Datun Nature Park.

   陽明山國家公園有很多具特色的觀光景點，例如大屯自然公園。

2. Ximending is a shopping district and it attracts many shoppers.

   西門町是個商店區，吸引了很多購物者。

3. Taroko National Park is one of the eight national parks in Taiwan.

   太魯閣國家公園是台灣八大國家公園之一。

4. Sun Moon Lake is the largest lake in Taiwan.

   日月潭是台灣最大的湖。

5. Alishan is famous for the sunrise view and the cloud ocean.

   阿里山的日出和雲海很有名。

單字、片語、句型解說

1. feature [ˈfitʃɚ]

▶ (動詞) 以…為特色

【三態：feature/featured/featured】

例 The movie features my favorite actress.

這部電影由我最喜歡的女演員主演。

2. tourist [ˈturɪst]

▶ (形容詞) 觀光的，旅遊的

例 You can find tourist information in this website.

你可以在這個網站上找到旅遊的資訊。

3. such as [sʌtʃ] [æz]

▶ (介係詞片語) 例如…

例 You should eat healthy foods, such as fruits and vegetables.

你應該吃健康的食物，例如水果跟蔬菜。

4. district [ˈdɪstrɪkt]

▶ (名詞) 地區

例 Taipei has many shopping districts.

台北有很多商店區。

●5. attract [ə`trækt]

▶ (動詞) 吸引

【三態：attract/attracted/attracted】

例 Your voice attracts me so much.
你的聲音是如此吸引我。

●6. shopper [`ʃɑpɚ]

▶ (名詞) 購物者

●7. lake [lek]

▶ (名詞) 湖

●8. sunrise [`sʌn,raɪz]

▶ (名詞) 日出

例 I enjoyed Alishan's sunrise.
我喜歡阿里山的日出。

●9. view [vju]

▶ (名詞) 景色

例 What a fine view of Sun Moon Lake!
日月潭的美麗風光真令人讚嘆！

●10. cloud [klaʊd]

▶ (名詞) 雲

●11. ocean [`oʃən]

▶ (名詞) 海洋

►►►► *6.* 台灣名產、紀念品
(Taiwan's special products & souvenirs)

相關用語

1. We can spend the whole afternoon buying souvenirs.

   整個下午我們都可以來買紀念品。

2. This market sells special products at discounted prices.

   在這市場可以買到打折的名產。

3. Taiwan offers local special products, each unique to its own area.

   台灣各地都有其道地獨特的名產。

4. Pineapple cakes, yolk pastries, and mung bean and meat pastries are all very tasty.

   鳳梨酥、蛋黃酥跟綠豆椪都非常美味。

5. You can buy suncakes in Taichung.

   在台中你可以買太陽餅。

6. You can buy many souvenirs in memory of your trip.

您可以買很多紀念品作為旅行留念。

單字、片語、句型解說

● 1. spend [spɛnd]

▶ (動詞) 花費 【三態：spend/spent/spent】

例 I spent two hours watching TV.
我花了兩個小時看電視。

● 2. whole [hol]

▶ (形容詞) 整個的

例 He spent the whole afternoon sleeping.
他整個下午都在睡覺。

● 3. souvenir [ˋsuvəˏnɪr]

▶ (名詞) 紀念品

例 Would you like to buy souvenirs with me?
你想跟我去買紀念品嗎？

4. special products [ˈspɛʃəl] [ˈprɑdəkts]

▶ (名詞片語) 名產

例 This shop offers special products of Taiwan.

這家店販賣台灣名產。

 MP3 039

5. discounted [ˈdɪskaʊntɪd]

▶ (形容詞) 打折的

例 It's so lucky to buy this bag at a discounted price.

能以折扣價買到這個袋子真幸運。

6. price [praɪs]

▶ (名詞) 價格

例 What's the price of this car?

這部車多少錢？

7. unique [juˈnik]

▶ (形容詞) 獨特的

例 You have such a unique voice.

你的嗓子如此獨特。

8. pineapple cakes [ˈpaɪnˌæp!] [keks]

▶ (名詞片語) 鳳梨酥

例 Where can I buy pineapple cakes?

在哪可以買到鳳梨酥？

●9. yolk pastries [jok] [ˋpestrɪz]

▶ (名詞片語) 蛋黃酥

例 Buy me two boxes of yolk pastries.
給我買兩盒蛋黃酥。

●10. mung bean and meat pastries [mʌŋ] [bin] [ænd] [mit] [ˋpestrɪz]

▶ (名詞片語) 綠豆椪

例 My father likes to eat mung bean and meat pastries.
我爸爸喜歡吃綠豆椪。

●11. suncakes [ˋsʌn͵keks]

▶ (名詞) 太陽餅

例 Suncakes are originally from the city of Taichung in Taiwan.
太陽餅源自於台灣台中。

●12. in memory of [ɪn] [ˋmɛmərɪ] [ɑv]

▶ (介係詞片語) 用以紀念…

例 We will build a museum in memory of the artist.
我們會蓋一座博物館來紀念這位藝術家。

台灣常見紀念品

紀念品中文名	對照之英文及音標	組成的單字解說
茶具	tea sets [ti] [sɛts]	tea (名詞)茶 se (名詞)一套，一副
油紙傘	oil-paper umbrella [ɔɪl] [ˋpepɚ] [ʌmˋbrɛlə]	oil-paper (形容詞)油紙的 umbrella(名詞)雨傘
竹製品	bamboo-made items [bæmˋbu] [med] [ˋaɪtəmz]	bamboo-made (形容詞)竹製的 item(名詞)項目，品目
印有中國字的物品	items with Chinese characters [ˋaɪtəmz] [wɪð] [ˋtʃaɪˋniz] [ˋkærɪktɚz]	item(名詞)項目，品目 with(介係詞)有 Chinese (形容詞)中國的 character (名詞)文字
書法畫卷	calligraphy scrolls [ˌkælɪˋgræfɪk] [skrolz]	calligraphy (形容詞)書法的 scroll(名詞)畫卷

❶ 工作場合

MP3 041

Lesson 5

送機
(To See Someone Off)

　　在經歷了一連串的參訪行程後,為了讓客戶有賓至如歸的感覺,並留下深刻的美好回憶,最後的接送行程也是不可疏忽的。一般而言,需事先替客戶安排交通車至飯店接送,經過了幾天的接待及陪伴,在乘坐交通車時,想必也會比第一天接機見面時,有更多的話想說,可以把握機會在車上好好聊聊。最後,在抵達機場的時候,除了幫忙引導辦理登機前的手續,在入關說再見前如能致贈準備好的紀念品,並同時表達對客戶專程前來參與所有行程的感謝,相信一定能讓接待的任務畫下完美的句點。

引言的關鍵單字或片語:

1. feel at home [fil] [æt] [hom]
   (動詞片語)感覺自在,賓至如歸

2. memory [`mɛmərɪ]　　　(名詞)記憶,回憶

3. see off [si] [ɔf]　　　(動詞片語)替…送行

4. reception [rɪ`sɛpʃən]　　(名詞)接待

5. keep company with [kip] [`kʌmpənɪ]
[wɪð] +人　　　　　(動詞片語)陪伴某人

6. vehicle [`viɪk!]　(名詞)交通工具，
車輛

7. seize the chance [siz] [ðə] [tʃæns]
(動詞片語)把握機會

8. arrive [ə`raɪv]+in 大地方/ at 小地方
(動詞片語)抵達…

9. flight [flaɪt]　　　(名詞)飛行

10. souvenir [`suvə͵nɪr]　(名詞)紀念品

11. gratitude [`grætəˏtjud] (名詞)感激

12. a perfect ending [ə] [`pɝfɪkt] [`ɛndɪŋ]
(名詞片語)完美的句點，完美的結束

MP3 042

1. 至飯店接送
(picking the clients up at the hotel)

相關用語

1. I will pick you up at the hotel at 10:00 a.m. tomorrow.
   明天早上十點我會去飯店接你。

2. I will drive you to the airport.
   我會開車載你去機場。

3. This way! A taxi is waiting for us.
   請往這邊走！計程車在等我們。

4. Did you bring all of your belongings?
   您的東西都帶齊了嗎？

5. Did you check everything before you left?
   您在離開前檢查了所有東西了嗎？

6. Are you all ready?
   一切都準備妥當了嗎？

7. We will pay for the hotel and the plane tickets for you.
   我們會替您付飯店及機票的錢。

單字、片語、句型解說

1. drive [draɪv]

▶ (動詞) 開車送...人

【三態：drive/drove/driven】

例 You should drive the client to the airport.

你應該開車送客戶去機場。

2. airport [`ɛr͵port]

▶ (名詞) 機場

例 You can buy duty-free products at the airport.

你可以在機場買免稅商品。

3. bring [brɪŋ]

▶ (動詞) 帶來 【三態：bring/brought/brought】

例 Don't forget to bring your glasses.

別忘了帶眼鏡來。

4. belongings [bə`lɔŋɪŋz]

▶ (名詞) 財產，攜帶物品

例 All of these are your belongings.

這所有的東西都是你的。

工作場合

MP3 043

●5. check [tʃɛk]

▶ (動詞) 檢查 【三態：check/checked/checked】

例 Did you check the gas before you left?

你在離開前有檢查瓦斯嗎？

●6. leave [liv]

▶ (動詞) 離開 【三態：leave/left/left】

例 She left the classroom at noon.

她在中午時離開教室。

●7. plane [plen]

▶ (名詞) 飛機

例 Have you ever been on a plane?

你搭過飛機嗎？

●8. ticket [`tɪkɪt]

▶ (名詞) 票

例 Please show me your ticket.

請把票拿給我看一下。

2. 乘坐交通工具時
(in the vehicles)

相關用語

1. I wish you could stay longer.
   但願您能待久一點。

2. There are still many things you haven't seen.
   您還有很多東西沒見識到。

3. There are still many places you haven't visited.
   您還有很多地方沒去參觀。

4. It was great to spend time with you the past few days.
   過去這幾天跟您相處得非常開心。

5. What was your favorite part of the trip?
   這次旅行您最喜歡的是哪一部分？

6. I am so glad to see the progress our two companies have made.

很高興見到我們兩家公司所做的進展。

7. Would you like to call anyone to say goodbye?

您想要打電話給誰道別嗎？

 MP3 044

單字、片語、句型解說

● 1. wish [wɪʃ]

▶ (動詞) 希望

【假設語氣，表示與事實相反的設想】

例 I wish I were healthy.

但願我是健康的。

● 2. could [kʊd]

▶ (助動詞) (用於假設語氣，表示與事實相反的設想)能，可以

例 I wish I could buy a new car.

但願我能買新車。

● 3. stay [ste]

▶ (動詞) 停留 【三態：stay/stayed/stayed】

例 I will stay here for two hours.

我會在這裡待兩小時。

4. long [bɒŋ]

▶ (形容詞) 長久的

【longer為副詞比較級，意思為「更久的」】

例 I hope to stay at the hotel longer.
我希望可以在飯店待更久一點。

5. still [stɪl]

▶ (副詞) 仍然

例 He still loves you.
他還愛著你。

6. see [si]

▶ (動詞) 看見 【三態：see/saw/seen】

這邊是have+pp，seen是過去分詞(pp)

例 I haven't seen her for a long time.
我好久沒看到她了。

7. spend [spɛnd]

▶ (動詞) 花費 【三態：spend/spent/spent】

例 I like to spend time with my dogs.
我喜歡花時間跟我的狗在一起。

8. past [pæst]

▶ (形容詞) 過去的

例 Over the past few days, we have visited many places.
過去幾天我們已經參觀了許多地方。

●9. part [pɑrt]

▶ (名詞) 部分

例 What's your favorite part of this film?
這部電影你最喜歡哪一個部分？

MP3 045

●10. trip [trɪp]

▶ (名詞) 旅行

例 She will go on a business trip next month.
下個月她將出差。

●11. glad [glæd]

▶ (形容詞) 高興的

例 I am so glad to meet you today.
很高興今天能夠見到你。

●12. progress [`prɑgrɛs]

▶ (名詞) 進展

例 I hope to make great progress this year.
我希望今年能夠大有進步。

3. 抵達機場
(when arriving at the airport)

相關用語

1. When is your flight?
   您的班機是幾點？

2. When is the expected arrival time?
   預計抵達時間是何時？

3. Will someone pick you up after you arrive in Japan?
   抵達日本後，有人會來接您嗎？

4. Let me help you with the luggage.
   讓我來幫您拿行李。

5. I suggest you try the Hilton Hotel after you arrive in Hong Kong.
   抵達香港後，我建議您試試希爾頓飯店。

6. Hope you enjoy your stay in London.
   希望您在倫敦順心愉快。

7. I hope you will have a good flight.
   希望您一路順風。

單字、片語、句型解說

● 1. flight [flaɪt]

▶ (名詞) 班次

例 What is your flight number?
您的班機號碼為何？

● 2. expected [ɪk`spɛktɪd]

▶ (形容詞) 期待中的

例 She arrived earlier than the expected time.
她比預定的時間早到。

● 3. arrival [ə`raɪv!]

▶ (名詞) 到達

● 4. arrive [ə`raɪv]

▶ (動詞) 到達　【三態：arrive/arrived/arrived】

● 5. luggage [`lʌgɪdʒ]

▶ (名詞) 行李

● 6. suggest [sə`dʒɛst]

▶ (動詞) 建議

　【三態：suggest/suggested/suggested】

例 He suggested that I drink more water.
他建議我多喝水。

4. 登機前的手續
(check in before the flight)

相關用語

1. You should check in at least one hour before departure.

   您應該在至少一小時前辦理登機。

2. May I have your ticket and passport?

   我可以看一下您的機票跟護照嗎？

3. Do you have any luggage to check in?

   您有任何行李要托運嗎？

4. Do you just have one piece of luggage to check in?

   您只有一件行李要托運嗎？

5. Your luggage is over the limit. You have to pay an extra charge.

   您的行李超重。您必須付額外的費用。

6. Do you have anything to declare?

   您有任何東西要申報嗎？

單字、片語、句型解說

●1. check in [tʃɛk] [ɪn]

▶ (動詞片語) 登機，托運

例 How early do I need to check in for my flight?

我需要多早辦理登機？

例 She has two pieces of luggage to check in.

她有兩件行李要托運。

●2. at least [æt] [list]

▶ (介係詞片語) 至少

例 I drink at least three glasses of water a day.

我一天至少喝三杯水。

●3. passport [`pæs͵port]

▶ (名詞) 護照

例 I need to apply for a passport.

我需要申請護照。

●4. piece [pis]

▶ (名詞) 一個，一件，一張

例 I need three pieces of paper.

我需要三張紙。

5. over [`ovɚ]

▸ (介係詞) 超過

例 There are over 20 people in the classroom.
超過二十人在教室裡。

6. limit [`lɪmɪt]

▸ (名詞) 限制

例 You should know your own limits.
你最好有自知之明。

7. extra [`ɛkstrə]

▸ (形容詞) 額外的

例 Do you need any extra help?
您需要任何額外的幫助嗎？

8. charge [tʃɑrdʒ]

▸ (名詞) 收費

例 The admission charge is NTD 100.
入場費是一百元台幣。

9. declare [dɪ`klɛr]

▸ (動詞) 申報

【三態：declare/declared/declared】

例 He has nothing to declare.
他沒什麼要申報的。

5. 致贈紀念品
(presenting the clients with souvenirs)

相關用語

1. I have a souvenir for you.
   我有一個紀念品要給您。

2. I want you to have this.
   我有東西要請您收下。

3. This is an exclusive business souvenir for you.
   這是給您的獨家商業紀念品。

4. This is a souvenir to remember your trip by.
   這是一個能讓您回憶起這趟旅程的紀念品。

5. You can open it on the plane.
   您可以在飛機上打開來看。

6. I hope you will like it.
   希望您會喜歡。

7. These are gifts for your family.
   這些是給您家人的禮物。

單字、片語、句型解說

1. souvenir [ˈsuvəˌnɪr]

▶ (名詞) 紀念品

例 I need to buy some souvenirs for my friends.
我需要買一些紀念品給我朋友。

2. exclusive [ɪkˈsklusɪv]

▶ (形容詞) 獨家的，獨有的

例 I hope to have an exclusive interview with the president.
我希望能獨家採訪總裁。

3. remember+事物+by

▶ 【回憶起…事物】

例 I hope to buy something to remember my trip by.
我希望買一些能讓我回憶起這趟旅程的東西。

4. can [kæn]

▶ (助動詞) 可以

例 Can I use your computer?
我可以用你的電腦嗎？

MP3 049

●5. open [`opən]

▶ (動詞) 打開 【三態：open/opened/opened】

例 Please open the windows.
請把窗戶打開。

●6. plane [plen]

▶ (名詞) 飛機

例 You can sleep on the plane.
你可以在飛機上睡覺。

●7. gift [gɪft]

▶ (名詞) 禮物

例 This is your birthday gift.
這是你的生日禮物。

●8. family [`fæməlɪ]

▶ (名詞) 家庭，家人

例 I love my family.
我愛我的家人。

6. 表達感謝
(expressing gratitude)

相關用語

1. I really enjoyed our time together.
   我真的很享受一起共渡的時光。

2. I hope you enjoyed your trip this time.
   我希望您會喜歡這次的旅行。

3. I am glad that we joined in a lot of
   activities together.
   我很高興我們一起參加了很多的活動。

4. I think we made the most of our time.
   我想我們妥善地利用了時間。

5. Please accept this gift for your
   patience and support.
   為了感謝您的耐心及支持，請收下這份禮物。

6. Thank you so much for all your help
   and participation.
   非常感謝您所有的協助及參與。

單字、片語、句型解說

● 1. enjoy [ɪnˋdʒɔɪ]

▶ (動詞) 享受 【三態：enjoy/enjoyed/enjoyed】

例 I really enjoyed this song.
我真的喜歡這首歌。

● 2. this time [ðɪs] [taɪm]

▶ (副詞片語) 這一次

例 He was really angry this time.
他這一次真的很生氣。

● 3. join in [dʒɔɪn] [ɪn]

▶ (動詞片語) 參加

例 I am going to join in the meeting.
我將參加會議。

● 4. activity [ækˋtɪvətɪ]

▶ (名詞) 活動

例 Singing is my favorite activity.
唱歌是我最喜歡的活動。

● 5. make the most of [mek] [ðə] [most] [ɑv]

▶ (動詞片語) 充分利用

例 You should make the most of your time.
你應該充分利用你的時間。

●6. accept [əkˋsɛpt]

▶ (動詞) 接受

【三態：accept/accepted/accepted】

例 Please accept my apology.
請接受我的道歉。

●7. patience [ˋpeʃəns]

▶ (名詞) 耐心

例 You need a lot of patience to be a good teacher.
要成為好老師，你需要很多耐心。

●8. support [səˋport]

▶ (名詞) 支持

例 He needs my support.
他需要我的支持。

●9. thank+人+for+事

▶ 【因為…而感謝…人】

例 I really thank you for your help.
我真的很感謝你的協助。

●10. participation [pɑr͵tɪsəˋpeʃən]

▶ (名詞) 參與

例 We need your participation.
我們需要您的參與。

7. 道別
(saying goodbye)

相關用語

1. I guess this is goodbye.
   我想我們真的要說再見了。

2. Hope you will come to visit us soon.
   希望您很快就會來拜訪我們。

3. Don't forget to keep in touch.
   別忘了要保持聯繫喔。

4. I really hope we can have more time.
   真希望我們還有更多的時間。

5. I look forward to seeing you again.
   期待下次與您相見。

6. Have a safe flight!
   祝旅途平安！

7. Bye-bye. Take care!
   再見了，保重！

單字、片語、句型解說

●1. guess [gɛs]

▶ (動詞) 猜測 【三態：guess/guessed/guessed】

例 Can you guess her age?
你猜得出來她幾歲嗎？

●2. visit [ˈvɪzɪt]

▶ (動詞) 拜訪 【三態：visit/visited/visited】

例 I hope to visit you next week.
下週我希望能拜訪你。

●3. keep in touch [kip] [ɪn] [tʌtʃ]

▶ (動詞片語) 保持聯繫

例 Let's keep in touch!
要保持聯繫喔！

●4. safe [sef]

▶ (形容詞) 平安的，安全的

例 I feel safe with him.
跟他在一起我覺得有安全感。

Chapter

2

學習場合
(On Learning Occasions)

Lesson 1
學校語言教室
(Language Classrooms at Schools)

　　因應台灣國際化的大環境，不論在公立或私立，日間或夜間，小學、中學、大學、社會人士，外籍老師在學校的語言教室裡授課已是常見的現象。

　　而在台灣的課堂上，也會有來自不同國家、文化、年齡、教育體系的外籍生，他們的參與不僅僅帶來思想文化的衝擊，也帶來語言差異的溝通磨合。在這樣國際化的教室環境裡，擁有好的英文溝通能力，就等於擁有了學習上取得高分、人際互動上取得優勢的條件，並能替課堂學習帶來愉悅的經驗。

❷ 學習場合

引言的關鍵單字或片語：

1. international [ˌɪntɚˋnæʃənl̩]
   (形容詞)國際的

2. environment [ɪnˋvaɪrənmənt]
   (名詞)環境

3. a foreign language teacher [ə] [ˋfɔrɪn]
   [ˋlæŋgwɪdʒ] [ˋtitʃɚ] (名詞片語)外籍語言老師

4. a language classroom [ə] [ˋlæŋgwɪdʒ]
   [ˋklæsˏrʊm]　　　　(名詞片語)語言教室

5. a foreign student [ə] [ˋfɔrɪn] [ˋstjudənt]
   　　　　　　　　　(名詞片語)外籍生

6. difference [ˋdɪfərəns]　　(名詞)差異

7. communication [kəˏmjunəˋkeʃən]
   　　　　　　　　　(名詞)溝通

8. run-in [ˋrʌnɪn]　　　　(名詞)吵架，磨合

9. ability [əˋbɪlətɪ]　　　　(名詞)能力

10. learning experience [ˋlɜnɪŋ] [ɪkˋspɪrɪəns]
    　　　　　　　　　(名詞片語)學習經驗

053

1. 自我介紹(學習背景)
(self-introduction: educational background)

相關用語

1. My name is Jessica. What's your name?
   我叫潔西卡。你呢?

2. I am from Taiwan.
   我來自台灣。

3. I am 29 years old.
   我二十九歲。

4. I am a salesman at a computer company.
   我是一家電腦公司的推銷員。

5. I majored in computers at college.
   大學時我主修電腦。

6. I have studied English for six years.
   我學英文已經六年了。

7. I passed the intermediate level of the General English Proficiency Test last year.
   去年我已經通過全民英檢中級檢定考。

❷ 學習場合

單字、片語、句型解說

●1. from [frɑm]

▶ (介係詞) 來自於

例 He comes from Tainan.
他來自台南。

●2. old [old]

▶ (形容詞) 老的，…歲的

例 How old are you?
你幾歲？

●3. salesman [`selzmən]

▶ (名詞) 推銷員

例 The salesman is showing her new computers.
推銷員正在向她展示新電腦。

●4. major in [`medʒɚ] [ɪn]

▶ (動詞片語) 主修…

例 I major in English.
我主修英文。

●5. college [`kɑlɪdʒ]

▶ (名詞) 大學，學院

例 I plan to study abroad after college.
大學畢業後我打算出國唸書。

054

●6. learn [lɝn]

▶ (動詞) 學習 【三態：learn/learned/learned】

這邊是「現在完成式：have+pp」，learned是過去分詞(pp)

例 Tom is learning Japanese now.
湯姆正在學日文。

●7. had passed 為 had+過去分詞(pp)

▶ 為「過去完成式」的用法。

pass [pæs]

(動詞)通過 【三態：pass/passed/passed】

例 I hope to pass the important exam next week.
我希望能通過下週重要的考試。

●8. intermediate [ˌɪntɚˋmidɪət]

▶ (形容詞) 中級的

●9. level [ˋlɛvl]

▶ (名詞) 程度

intermediate level [ˌɪntɚˋmidɪət] [ˋlɛvl]
(名詞片語) 中級

●10. the General English Proficiency Test
[ðə] [ˋdʒɛnərəl] [ˋɪŋglɪʃ] [prəˋfɪʃənsɪ] [tɛst]

▶ (名詞片語) 全民英檢，簡稱「GEPT」

②
學習場合

2. 學習動機
(learning motivation)

相關用語

1. I need to improve my English to do a better job.
   我需要改善英文以增進工作能力。

2. I need to learn English to find a good job.
   我需要學英文以找到好工作。

3. I hope to get better grades on English tests.
   我希望英文考試能拿到更好的分數。

4. I hope to pass the elementary level of the General English Proficiency Test.
   我希望能夠通過全民英檢初級的考試。

5. I want to study abroad next year.
   明年我要出國念書。

6. I like to make friends with foreigners.
   我喜歡跟外國人交朋友。

055

單字、片語、句型解說

●1. improve [ɪmˋpruv]

▷ (動詞) 改善

【三態：improve/improved/improved】

例 I don't know how to improve my English.

我不知道如何改善我的英文。

●2. do a better job

▷ (動詞片語) 把工作做得更好

【good(好的)→ better(更好的)→ best(最好的)，所以better是形容詞比較級，意思是「更好的」】

●3. find [faɪnd]

▷ (動詞) 發現，找到

【三態：find/found/found】

例 I can't find my wallet.

我找不到我的錢包。

❷ 學習場合

●4. grade [gred]

▶ (名詞) 分數

例 He got a low grade on the math test yesterday.

昨天的數學考試他得低分。

●5. elementary [ˌɛləˋmɛntərɪ]

▶ (形容詞) 基礎的，初級的

elementary level [ˌɛləˋmɛntərɪ] [ˋlɛv!]

(名詞片語)初級

例 I have to pass the elementary level of the GEPT by 2013.

二〇一三年前我必須通過全民英檢初級的考試。

●6. abroad [əˋbrɔd]

▶ (副詞) 到國外，在國外

例 My younger brother is studying abroad.

我弟正在國外念書。

●7. foreigner [ˋfɔrɪnə]

▶ (名詞) 外國人

例 There are many foreigners in Taipei.

台北有很多外國人。

3. 學習目標
(learning objectives)

相關用語

1. I can learn how to introduce myself.
   我可以學會如何自我介紹。

2. I can learn to talk about my feelings.
   我可以學著去述說自己的感覺。

3. I can know how to express my opinions.
   我可以知道如何表達自己的意見。

4. I can know how to interact with others.
   我可以知道如何與別人互動。

5. I can learn to communicate with my clients in English.
   我可以學會用英文跟我的客戶溝通。

6. I can learn now to write English e-mails to foreign customers.
   我可以學會寫英文電子郵件給國外的客戶。

7. I can learn how to write and read English letters.

我可以學會如何讀寫英文信。

單字、片語、句型解說

●1. introduce [ˌɪntrəˋdjus]

▶ (動詞) 介紹

【三態：introduce/introduced/introduced】

例 Please introduce yourself first.

請先介紹您自己。

●2. feelings [ˋfilɪŋz]

▶ (名詞) 感覺

例 What are your feelings about your new car?

你對你的新車的感覺如何？

●3. express [ɪkˋsprɛs]

▶ (動詞) 表達

【三態：express/expressed/expressed】

例 I don't know how to express my feeling.

我不知道如何表達我的感受。

4. opinion [ə`pɪnjən]

▶ (名詞) 意見

例 What is your opinion on this issue?
你對這個議題的意見為何?

MP3 057

5. interact [ˌɪntəˈækt]

▶ (動詞) 互動

【三態:interact/interacted/interacted】

例 I like to interact with people.
我喜歡與人互動。

❷ 學習場合

6. communicate [kəˈmjunəˌket]

▶ (動詞) 溝通,交流

【三態:communicate/communicated/
communicated】

例 I study English in order to communicate.
我學英文是為了與人溝通。

7. client [ˈklaɪənt]

▶ (名詞) 客戶

例 David is an important client of my company.
大衛是我的公司一位重要的客戶。

8. write [raɪt]

▶ (動詞) 寫 【三態：write/wrote/written】

例 I can write in English.
我會寫英文。

9. foreign [ˋfɔrɪn]

▶ (形容詞) 外國的

例 I like to make friends with foreign students.
我喜歡跟外籍學生交朋友。

10. customer [ˋkʌstəmɚ]

▶ (名詞) 顧客

例 Be nice to your customers!
要善待你的客戶！

11. read [rid]

▶ (動詞) 讀 【三態同形】

例 He is reading a book.
他正在讀一本書。

4. 描述學校
(school description)

相關用語

1. My school is very big and beautiful.
   我的學校很大又很美。

2. There are about fifty teachers and one thousand students in my school.
   我的學校大約有五十個老師和一千個學生。

3. There are many modern teaching buildings at my school.
   我的學校裡面有很多現代化的教學大樓。

4. Many students like to borrow books at the school library.
   許多學生喜歡在學校的圖書館裡借書。

5. Many students play basketball and volleyball in the big playground.
   許多學生在大運動場裡打籃球跟排球。

6. My school is a modern school in Taipei.
   我的學校是位於台北的一所現代化的學校。

工作場合 ❶

學習場合 ❷

朋友場合 ❸

單字、片語、句型解說

● 1. there+be 動詞(are 或 were)+ 複數名詞+地點

▶ 【在…地方有…】

例 There are many animals in this zoo.
這個動物園裡面有很多動物。

● 2. fifty [ˈfɪftɪ]

▶ (名詞) 五十

例 My father is fifty years old.
我父親五十歲。

● 3. thousand [ˈθaʊzənd]

▶ (名詞) 一千

例 This bag costs one thousand dollars.
這個袋子一千元。

● 4. modern [ˈmɑdən]

▶ (形容詞) 現代的

例 I live in a modern building.
我住在現代化的大樓裡。

● 5. teaching buildings [ˈtitʃɪŋ] [ˈbɪldɪŋz]

▶ (名詞片語) 教學大樓

例 How many teaching buildings are there in your school?
你的學校有幾棟教學大樓？

•6. borrow [`baro]

▸ (動詞) 借

【三態：borrow/borrowed/borrowed】

例 Can I borrow some money from you?
我可以跟你借點錢嗎？

•7. library [`laɪ,brɛrɪ]

▸ (名詞) 圖書館

例 I borrowed a book from the school library yesterday.
昨天我從學校圖書館裡借了一本書。

•8. playground [`ple,graʊnd]

▸ (名詞) 運動場

例 He enjoys jogging on the playground.
他喜歡在操場慢跑。

5. 學習經驗
(learning experience)

相關用語

1. I didn't enjoy learning English in the past.
   以前我不喜歡學英文。

2. I was a slow learner, but I studied hard.
   我學得很慢，但是我很用功。

3. It was hard for me to memorize English vocabulary.
   背英文單字對我來說是困難的。

4. Sometimes I fell asleep during the class.
   有時候我在上課時睡著。

5. I even decided to give it up.
   我甚至決定要放棄。

6. With my teacher's help, I can speak English very well now.
   在老師的協助之下，我現在英文說得很好。

7. I'd like to share my experience of learning English with you.

我想要跟你們分享我學習英文的經驗。

 060

單字、片語、句型解說

●1. in the past [ɪn] [ðə] [pæst]

► (介係詞片語) 在過去

例 He didn't want to talk to me in the past.

過去他不願意跟我說話。

●2. slow learner [slo] [lɝnɚ]

► (名詞片語) 緩慢的學習者

例 A good teacher has to be patient with slow learners.

好老師對緩慢的學習者必須要有耐心。

●3. hard [hɑrd]

► (副詞) 努力地

例 She studies hard every day.

她每天都很用功讀書。

●4. hard [hɑrd]

▶ (形容詞) 困難的

例 It's hard for me to sing in English.
用英文唱歌對我而言是困難的。

●5. memorize [`mɛmə,raɪz]

▶ (動詞) 背熟

【三態：memorize/memorized/memorized】

例 Can you memorize all the new words?
你可以把這些所有新的單字都記住嗎？

●6. vocabulary [və`kæbjə,lɛrɪ]

▶ (名詞) 字彙

例 Reading will increase your vocabulary.
閱讀會增加你的單字量。

●7. fall asleep [fɔl] [ə`slip]

▶ (動詞片語) 睡著　【三態：fall/fell/fallen】

例 Do you often fall asleep during the class?
你常在上課中睡著嗎？

●8. decide to [dɪ`saɪd] [tu]+原形動詞

▶ 【決定…】

【三態：decide/decided/decided】

例 I decided to move to Kaohsiung.
我決定要搬到高雄。

●9. give up [gɪv] [ʌp]

▶ (動詞片語) 放棄

例 Don't give up so easily!
不要那麼容易就放棄！

MP3 061

●10. with [wɪð]

▶ (介係詞) 有…

例 With your help, I can make more progress.
有了你的幫助，我可以更進步。

●11. share [ʃɛr]

▶ (動詞) 分享 【三態：share/shared/shared】

例 He shares a room with his younger brother.
他跟他弟弟合住一間房間。

●12. experience [ɪkˋspɪrɪəns]

▶ (名詞) 經驗

例 I have no experience of teaching Japanese.
我沒有教日文的經驗。

6. 與外籍師生互動
(interacting with foreign teachers and students)

相關用語

1. May I call you Helen?
   我可以叫你海倫嗎？

2. Is this your first time in Taipei?
   這是你第一次來台北嗎？

3. Are you here for long?
   你會在這待很久嗎？

4. You are a very interesting person.
   你真是一個非常有趣的人。

5. Your class is very easy and interesting.
   你的課很容易又有趣。

6. Can you teach me how to pronounce this word?
   你可以教我這個字的發音嗎？

7. I learn a lot from you. Thank you very much.
   我從你身上學到很多。非常謝謝。

單字、片語、句型解說

1. may [me]

▶ (助動詞) (表示許可或請求許可) 可以

例 May I talk to your teacher?
我可以跟你的老師聊聊嗎?

2. call+人+名字

▶ 【叫⋯人⋯名字】

例 We call him Michael.
我們叫他麥可。

3. for+一段時間 【表經歷了⋯的時間】
long [lɔŋ]

▶ (名詞) 長時間,長時期

例 She is not going away for long.
她不會離開太久。

4. interesting [ˋɪntərɪstɪŋ]

▶ (形容詞) 有趣的

例 This is an interesting story.
這是一個有趣的故事。

5. easy [ˋizɪ]

▶ (形容詞)容易的

例 Dancing is easy for me.
跳舞對我來說是容易的。

●6. teach [titʃ]

▶ (動詞) 教導 【三態：teach/taught/taught】

例 I'll teach you to dance.
我會教妳跳舞。

●7. pronounce [prə`naʊns]

▶ (動詞) 發音

【三態：pronounce/pronounced/pronounced】

例 She can pronounce the new words correctly.
她可以把這些新的單字都讀得很正確。

●8. from [frɑm]

▶ (介係詞) 從⋯

例 Where are you from?
你哪裡人？

▶▶▶▶ **7. 聯繫方式**
(contact information)

相關用語

1. Can I have your cell phone number?
   可以給我你的手機號碼嗎？

2. Do you have an e-mail address?
   你有電子郵件地址嗎？

3. Can you please tell me your address?
   你可以告訴我你的地址嗎？

4. Could we meet later this evening?
   稍後我們可以傍晚時見個面嗎？

5. Can I make an appointment with you for the test?
   為了這考試，我可以跟您約時間嗎？

6. Can we meet after class to discuss homework?
   下課後我們可以碰面討論功課嗎？

7. Would you like to go to the library with me after class?
   下課後你想和我一起去圖書館嗎？

❶ 工作場合
❷ 學習場合
❸ 朋友場合

單字、片語、句型解說

●1. number [ˈnʌmbɚ]

▶ (名詞) 號碼

例 Do you know her phone number?
你知道她的電話號碼嗎？

●2. address [əˈdrɛs]

▶ (名詞) 地址

例 You didn't write the address clearly.
你地址沒有寫清楚。

●3. later [ˈletɚ]

▶ (副詞) 稍後，晚點

例 I will call you later.
晚點我會打電話給你。

●4. appointment [əˈpɔɪntmənt]

▶ (名詞) 約會

例 I have an appointment with my teacher tonight.
今晚我和我的老師有約。

●5. after class [ˈæftɚ] [klæs]

▶ (介係詞片語) 下課後

例 What do you usually do after class?
下課後你通常做什麼？

●6. discuss [dɪ`skʌs]

▸ (動詞) 討論

　　【三態：discuss/discussed/discussed】

例 We can discuss it later.
　　我們可以稍後再討論。

●7. library [`laɪˌbrɛrɪ]

▸ (名詞) 圖書館

例 I go to the library twice a week.
　　我一個禮拜上圖書館兩次。

●8.【補充】通常得到聯繫方式最方便及
　　快速的方法，就是遞上一張名片，名片
　　的內容大約需要以下這些資訊：

▸ (1)公司商標 (the logo of the company)

　　(2)公司名稱(the name of the company)

　　(3)姓名 (name)

　　(4)職稱、頭銜(position or title)

　　(5)公司地址(the address of the company)

　　(6)電話號碼(telephone number)

　　(7)傳真號碼(fax number)

　　(8)電子郵箱(E-mail address)

❶ 工作場合　❷ 學習場合　❸ 朋友場合

MP3 065

Lesson 2

研討會
Symposiums / Seminars

研討會中常會有國外的專業人士或是學者的參與，因此懂得運用適當的英文溝通是必要的能力。

【註】：台灣的「研討會」常見的形式約有五種，如下表所示，標題及內容說明僅以symposiums/seminars代表之：

常見形式	英文及音標
演講	lecture [ˋlɛktʃɚ]
座談	panel discussion [ˋpæn!] [dɪˋskʌʃən]
研究會、專家討論會	seminar [ˋsɛmə͵nɑr]
論壇	forum [ˋforəm]
專題研討會	symposium [sɪmˋpozɪəm]

引言的關鍵單字或片語：

1. a highly competitive era [ə] [ˋhaɪlɪ] [kəmˋpɛtətɪv] [ˋɪrə] (名詞片語)高度競爭的時代

2. an industry symposium [æn] [ˋɪndəstrɪ] [sɪmˋpozɪəm] (名詞片語)產業研討會

3. an academic symposium [æn] [͵ækəˋdɛmɪk] [sɪmˋpozɪəm] (名詞片語)學術研討會

4. field [fild] (名詞)領域

5. professional [prəˋfɛʃən!] (名詞)專家

6. scholar [ˋskɑlɚ] (名詞)學者

1. 迎接
(greeting)

相關用語

1. Good morning, Ms. Hsu.
   許女士，早安。

2. I'm Eva. Nice to meet you.
   我是伊娃。很高興見到您。

3. How are you doing?
   您好嗎？

4. You look lost. Can I be of assistance?
   您看起來好像迷路了。需要我幫忙嗎？

5. You're not from around here. Are you an American?
   您不是這裡的人。您是美國人嗎？

6. The seminar venue is on the third floor. Please follow me.
   研究會場地在三樓。請跟我來。

7. Please take your seminar materials and take the elevator to the sixth floor.
   請拿一下研究會的資料，然後搭電梯到六樓。

❶ 工作場合

❷ 學習場合

❸ 朋友場合

單字、片語、句型解說

●1. look+形容詞

▶【看起來…】

⑩ The teacher looks very angry.
老師看起來很生氣。

●2. lost [lɔst]

▶ (形容詞) 迷失的

⑩ She is looking for her lost child.
她正在找她迷失的小孩。

●3. assistance [əˋsɪstəns]

▶ (名詞) 協助

●4. around [əˋraʊnd]

▶ (介係詞) 在…附近

⑩ I live around the park.
我住在公園附近。

●5. American [əˋmɛrɪkən]

▶ (名詞) 美國人

●6. seminar [ˋsɛmə͵nɑr]

▶ (名詞) 研究會，專家討論會

⑩ There is a seminar on international business this afternoon.
下午有一場國際商務的討論會。

•7. venue [ˋvɛnju]

▸ (名詞) 發生地，集合地

例 Excuse me, could you tell me where the seminar venue is?

不好意思，您可以告訴我研究會場地在哪裡嗎？

•8. third [θɝd]

▸ (形容詞) 第三的

例 I won third place.

我得到第三名。

•9. take [tek]

▸ (動詞) 拿，搭乘 【三態：take/took/taken】

例 Did you take my pen?

你拿走我的筆嗎？

例 I am going to take a bus.

我要去搭公車了。

•10. material [məˋtɪrɪəl]

▸ (名詞)材料，資料

•11. elevator [ˋɛləˌvetɚ]

▸ (名詞) 電梯

2. 流程說明
(procedure description)

相關用語

1. The symposium will last for two days.
   研討會將進行兩天。

2. It will include invited talks and panel discussions.
   研討會將包含了邀請講座跟小組討論。

3. If you have any suggestions, please contact our staff.
   如您有任何建議，請聯絡我們的工作人員。

4. You will receive the materials on the desk.
   你將在會議桌那裡拿到會議資料。

5. There will be 20-minute breaks between sessions.
   每個議程中間會休息二十分鐘。

6. Lunch boxes will be provided at noon.
   中午將提供便當。

單字、片語、句型解說

•1. symposium [sɪm`pozɪəm]

▶ (名詞) 研討會,座談會

•2. last [læst]

▶ (動詞) 延續 【三態:last/lasted/lasted】

例 How long will the class last?
課要上多久?

•3. include [ɪn`klud]

▶ (動詞) 包含

【三態:include/included/included】

例 The price includes both the cake and the coffee.
價錢包括蛋糕跟咖啡。

•4. an invited talk [æn] [ɪn`vaɪtɪd] [tɔk]

▶ (名詞片語) 邀請講座

•5. a panel discussion [ə] [`pæn!] [dɪ`skʌʃən]

▶ (名詞片語) 小組討論

•6. suggestion [sə`dʒɛstʃən]

▶ (名詞) 建議

例 Do you have any suggestions?
您有任何建議嗎?

① 工作場合

② 學習場合

③ 朋友場合

●7. staff [stæf]

▶ (名詞) 工作人員

例 The staff of the museum are excellent.

這間博物館的工作人員都是出類拔萃的。

●8. receive [rɪ`siv]

▶ (動詞) 收到

【三態：receive/received/received】

例 I didn't receive your letter.

我沒有收到你的信。

●9. session [`sɛʃən]

▶ (名詞) 會議，集會

例 We will discuss education in the second session.

我們會在第二個議程中討論教育。

●10. a lunch box [ə] [lʌntʃ] [bɑks]

▶ (名詞片語) 便當

●11. provide [prə`vaɪd]

▶ (動詞) 提供

【三態：provide/provided/provided】

例 The hotel will provide breakfast and dinner.

飯店會提供早餐跟晚餐。

▶▶▶ 3. 環境介紹
(environment description)

相關用語

1. The venue has five main levels.
   這個場地主要有五層樓。

2. The venue is air-conditioned throughout.
   這個場地全館空調流通。

3. The venue is a good place to host exhibitions.
   這個場地是舉行展覽的好地方。

4. The reception area is on the second floor.
   接待區在二樓。

5. There are 15 meeting rooms in total.
   總共有十五間會議室。

6. The seminar is to be held in the conference room on the second floor.
   研究會將在二樓的會議室舉行。

❶ 工作場合

❷ 學習場合

❸ 朋友場合

7. The symposium is held in the
university's conference center.

研討會在這所大學的會議中心舉行。

單字、片語、句型解說

●1. level [ˋlɛvl]

(名詞) 樓層

例 How many levels are there in the
building?

這棟大樓有幾層？

●2. air-conditioned [ˋɛrkənˏdɪʃənd]

(形容詞) 有空調的

例 All the classrooms are air-conditioned
at our school.

我們學校所有教室都有空調。

●3. throughout [θruˋaʊt]

(副詞) 處處

例 My house is not air-conditioned
throughout.

我的房子不是到處都有空調。

●4. host [host]

(動詞) 舉行 【三態：host/hosted/hosted】

例 I will host a dinner party at my house next week.
下周我將在我家舉行晚宴。

•5. exhibition [ˌɛksə`bɪʃən]

▸ (名詞) 展覽

例 I look forward to the painting exhibition at the museum.
我期待博物館的畫展。

•6. reception [rɪ`sɛpʃən]

▸ (名詞) 接待

例 Where is the hotel reception?
飯店的接待處在哪裡？

•7. a meeting room [ə] [`mitɪŋ] [rum]

▸ (名詞片語) 會議室

例 Excuse me, where is the meeting room?
不好意思，請問會議室在哪裡？

•8. in total [ɪn] [`tot!]

▸ (介係詞片語) 總共

例 Only 25 people in total came to the exhibition last week.
上週總共只有二十五人來看這個展覽。

工作場合

❷ 學習場合

朋友場合

●9. is to be held

▶ 這邊有表「未來」的意味，意思為「將被舉行」。

be動詞+to be pp(過去分詞)→為表未來的被動式

(動詞)「舉行」的三態為「hold/held/held」。

例 An exhibition is to be held next month near my house.
下個月在我家附近將有一個展覽。

例 His birthday party is to be held at a restaurant.
他的生日派對將在一家餐廳舉行。

●10. university [ˌjunəˋvɝˋsətɪ]

▶ (名詞) 大學

例 The university will hold a forum.
這所大學將舉辦論壇。

●11. a conference center [ə] [ˋkɑnfərəns] [ˋsɛntɚ]

▶ (名詞片語) 會議中心

例 Excuse me, how can I get to the conference center?
不好意思，請問會議中心怎麼走？

▶▶▶ **4.** 參加動機
(motivation for participation)

相關用語

1. I can meet several experts in a short amount of time.
   我可以在短期間跟數個專家碰面。

2. I can meet new people and share experiences.
   我可以跟新朋友見面並分享經驗

3. The seminar can give me useful content on the topic of computers.
   這個研討會可以讓我得到與電腦相關的有用內容。

4. I can learn new information from the presenters.
   我可以從演講者身上學到新的資訊。

5. I can get new product or service ideas in my industry.
   我可以得到所從事領域的新產品或服務訊息。

① 工作場合

② 學習場合

③ 朋友場合

單字、片語、句型解說

●1. expert [`ɛkspɚt]

▶ (名詞) 專家

例 He is an expert in computers.
他是電腦專家。

●2. amount [ə`maʊnt]

▶ (名詞) 數量

例 We just need a short amount of time.
我們只需要一點時間。

●3. useful [`jusfəl]

▶ (形容詞) 有用的

例 The information in this book is
useful.
這本書裡的資訊是有用的。

●4. content [`kantɛnt]

▶ (名詞) 內容

例 This book lacks content.
這本書的內容乏善可陳。

●5. topic [`tapɪk]

▶ (名詞) 主題

例 They have many topics to talk about.
他們有很多話題可聊。

●6. presenter [prɪˋzɛntɚ]

▶ (名詞) 報告者，演講者

例 Dr. Tseng was the presenter of this topic.

曾博士是這個主題的報告者。

●7. product [ˋprɑdəkt]

▶ (名詞) 產品

例 There are markets for our products.

我們的產品有市場需求。

●8. service [ˋsɝvɪs]

▶ (名詞) 服務

例 That restaurant is famous for its fine service.

那家餐廳以服務優良著稱。

●9. industry [ˋɪndəstrɪ]

▶ (名詞) 行業

例 Is our service industry expanding?

我們的服務業正蓬勃發展嗎？

① 工作場合

② 學習場合

③ 朋友場合

5. 心得分享
(experience sharing)

相關用語

1. I really gained a lot of knowledge in this seminar.
   我真的從這個研討會裡得到很多知識。

2. I am glad that I met many friends with the same interests.
   我很高興跟同行的許多朋友碰面。

3. This seminar helped me improve the knowledge of this subject.
   這次的研討會幫助我改善這個主題的知識。

4. For me, it's also a nice vacation in the hotel where the seminar took place.
   對我來說，我也在研討會舉行的飯店裡度過了美好的假期。

5. The cost for the seminar is really too high.
   研討會收取的費用真的太高了。

單字、片語、句型解說

●1. gain [gen]

▶ (動詞) 得到 【三態：gain/gained/gained】

例 I gained a lot from your class.
你的課讓我獲益良多。

●2. interest [`ɪntərɪst]

▶ (名詞) 利益，同行

例 I hope to meet friends with the same interests in the seminar.
我希望可以在這次研討會裡跟同行的朋友碰面。

●3. improve [ɪm`pruv]

▶ (動詞) 改善

【三態：improve/improved/improved】

例 Do you know how to improve English listening skills?
你知道如何改善英文聽力嗎？

●4. subject [`sʌbdʒɪkt]

▶ (名詞) 主題

例 Have you read any books on the subject?
你讀過任何關於這方面主題的書嗎？

❶ 工作場合

❷ 學習場合

❸ 朋友場合

●5. vacation [ve`keʃən]

▶ (名詞) 假期

例 They are on vacation in Hawaii.
他們正在夏威夷度假。

●6. take place [tek] [ples]

▶ (動詞片語) 發生

例 When will the concert take place?
音樂會何時舉行？

●7. cost [kɔst]

▶ (名詞) 費用

例 What is the cost for the class?
這門課的費用是多少？

●8. high [haɪ]

▶ (形容詞) 高的，昂貴的

例 Why is the cost for the class so high?
這門課的費用為什麼那麼貴？

Lesson 3
補習班
(Cram Schools)

在台灣，除了正規的學校教育之外，許多人也會上補習班去加強英文或其他的學科。走在路上，補習班隨處可見，課後補習的風氣十分興盛。

有些人補習是為了加強學校上課的科目，以求在升學路上能夠順利。有些人則為了學習在學校學不到的才藝，例如鋼琴、書法、繪畫等等。

不論學習動機為何，在當今多元化的學習環境裡，面對的可能也是多元化的師生及教材，因此擁有良好的英文溝通能力，自然能夠令學習過程更為順利愉快。

引言的關鍵單字或片語：

1. school education [skul] [ˌɛdʒʊˋkeʃən]
   (名詞片語)學校教育

2. subject [ˋsʌbdʒɪkt] (名詞)科目，學科

3. talent and skill [ˋtælənt] [ænd] [ˋskɪl]
   (名詞片語)才藝

4. motivation [ˌmotəˋveʃən] (名詞)動機

5. diverse [daɪˋvɝs] (形容詞)多樣的，多元的

6. a learning environment [ə] [ˋlɝnɪŋ]
   [ɪnˋvaɪrənmənt] (名詞片語)學習環境

① 工作場合
② 學習場合
③ 朋友場合

MP3 075

1. 學習背景
(learning background)

相關用語

1. I study at a community college.
   我在社區大學念書。

2. My company pays for my training.
   公司負擔我訓練的費用。

3. My colleague suggested this class for me.
   我的同事推薦我上這門課。

4. I go to Yamaha Music School every Sunday.
   每周日我都會去山葉音樂教室上課。

5. I go to an English cram school twice a week.
   每周我會去英文補習班上兩次課。

6. I like the mathematics classes at this popular cram school.
   我喜歡這家知名補習班的數學課。

7. I have studied Japanese for 3 years at Global Village.
   我在地球村學日文已經三年了。

單字、片語、句型解說

●1. community [kə`mjunətɪ]

► (名詞) 社區

例 I live in a nearby community.
我住在附近的一個社區。

●2. college [`kɑlɪdʒ]

► (名詞) 大學，學院

例 I study in a music college in Taipei.
我在台北的一間音樂學院唸書。

●3. training [`trenɪŋ]

► (名詞) 訓練

例 You need some language training.
你需要一些語言訓練。

●4. colleague [`kɑlig]

► (名詞) 同事

例 I learn a lot from my colleague.
我從同事身上學到很多。

●5. suggest [sə`dʒɛst]

▶ (動詞) 建議

【三態：suggest/suggested/suggested】

例 I suggest going to the movies tonight.
我建議晚上去看電影。

MP3 076

●6. a music school

▶ [ə] [`mjuzɪk] [skul]

(名詞片語) 音樂教室

例 There is a music school near my house.
我家附近有一家音樂教室。

●7. a cram school [ə] [kræm] [skul]

▶ (名詞片語) 補習班

例 Do you go to a cram school?
你有上補習班嗎？

●8. twice [twaɪs]

▶ (副詞) 兩次

例 I come to see her twice a week.
我一個禮拜去看她兩次。

●9. mathematics [ˌmæθəˋmætɪks]

▶ (名詞) 數學

例 Mathematics is my favorite subject.
數學是我最喜歡的科目。

●10. popular [ˋpɑpjələ˞]

▶ (形容詞)受歡迎的

例 Do you like popular songs?
你喜歡流行歌曲嗎?

●11. have learned

▶ 為現在完成式【have + pp(過去分詞= learned)】,表到目前為止的經驗,意思為「已經學了…」。

❶ 工作場合

❷ 學習場合

❸ 朋友場合

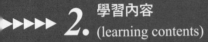

2. 學習內容
(learning contents)

相關用語

1. This class is meant to help you learn English listening skills.
   這門課是要幫助你學習英文聽力技能。

2. This class covers the basic steps in Waltz and Tango.
   這門課涵蓋了華爾滋跟探戈的基本舞步。

3. I come here to learn how to sing.
   我來這裡學唱歌。

4. This conversation class will last for 8 weeks.
   這門會話課將持續八週。

5. You are expected to submit homework assignments after class.
   你應繳交課後作業。

6. You can obtain guitar lessons on all levels at our music school.
   在我們的音樂教室裡你可以學到所有程度的吉他課。

單字、片語、句型解說

●1. be 動詞+meant [mɛnt]+to+V

▶ 【意思是⋯；打算要⋯】

mean/meant/meant，這邊用的是pp，為被動式。

例 This is meant to be a business trip.
這次是要出公差的。

●2. listening [ˈlɪsənɪŋ]

▶ (形容詞) 聽的

例 You may need to improve your listening skills.
你也許需要改善聽力技能。

●3. cover [ˈkʌvɚ]

▶ (動詞) 包含 【三態：cover/covered/covered】

例 This book covers many ideas.
這本書涵蓋許多想法。

●4. basic [ˈbesɪk]

▶ (形容詞) 基礎的，基本的

例 You need to learn basic skills.
你需要學習基本技能。

❶ 工作場合

❷ 學習場合

❸ 朋友場合

● 5. step [stɛp]

▶ (名詞) 腳步，舞步

● 6. conversation [ˌkɑnvɚˋseʃən]

▶ (名詞) 會話

例 Kevin is having a conversation with his teacher.
凱文正在跟他的老師對話。

● 7. submit [səbˋmɪt]

▶ (動詞) 繳交

【三態：submit/submitted/submitted】

例 When should I submit the assignment?
我什麼時候該交作業？

● 8. assignment [əˋsaɪnmənt]

▶ (名詞) 作業，功課

● 9. obtain [əbˋten]

▶ (動詞) 得到，獲得

【三態：obtain/obtained/obtained】

例 I am glad to obtain your contact information.
我很高興得到你的聯絡資料。

● 10. level [ˋlɛv!]

▶ (名詞) 程度

▶▶▶ **3.** 學習動機
(learning motivations)

相關用語

1. I hope to learn to play the piano.
   我希望學會彈鋼琴。

2. I need to improve my computer skills
   to find a job.
   我需要改善電腦技能以找到工作。

3. I like to keep fit by dancing.
   我喜歡藉由跳舞來維持身材。

4. I want to pass the TOEIC test this year.
   今年我想要通過多益考試。

5. I am interested in calligraphy, so I
   study it in a community college.
   我對書法感興趣，所以有去社區大學上課。

6. I may make friends with people who
   like music, too.
   也許我可以跟同樣喜歡音樂的人為友。

● 工作場合

❷ 學習場合

❸ 朋友場合

單字、片語、句型解說

●1. keep [kip]

▶ (動詞) 保持…

【三態：keep/kept/kept】

例 Exercise will help you keep healthy.
運動有益維持健康。

●2. fit [fɪt]

▶ (形容詞) 健康的，身材適中的

例 How can I look fit?
怎麼樣我才能擁有健美的身材？

●3. dance [dæns]

▶ (動詞) 跳舞

【三態：dance/danced/danced】

例 I enjoy dancing with you.
我喜歡跟你跳舞。

●4. so [so]

▶ (對等連接詞) 因此

例 I hope to keep fit, so I often exercise.
我希望維持好身材，所以我常常運動。

▶▶▶ *4.* 學習目標
(learning goals)

相關用語

1. I hope I can perform a solo dance.
   我希望我可以表演獨舞。

2. I hope I will not be afraid to sing in front of people.
   我希望我不會懼怕在人前唱歌。

3. I hope to create a good PowerPoint presentation.
   我希望製作出好的ppt簡報。

4. I hope I can learn to write beautiful calligraphy.
   我希望可以學會一手漂亮的書法。

5. I hope to be a professional pianist one day.
   我希望有一天可以成為專業的鋼琴家。

6. I hope I can hold a guitar concert one day.
   我希望有一天我可以舉辦吉他演奏會。

① 工作場合
❷ 學習場合
❸ 朋友場合

單字、片語、句型解說

●1. perform [pəˋfɔrm]

▶ (動詞) 表演

【三態：perform/performed/performed】

例 I am afraid to perform in front of people.
我害怕在人前表演。

●2. solo [ˋsolo]

▶ (形容詞) 獨奏的，獨唱的

例 This is a great solo performance.
這是一場很棒的獨秀。

●3. afraid [əˋfred]

▶ (形容詞) 害怕的，恐懼的

例 She is afraid to talk to me.
她不敢跟我說話。

●4. in front of [ɪn] [frʌnt] [ɑv]

▶ (介係詞片語) 在…前面

例 John is standing in front of me.
約翰正站在我前面。

•5. create [krɪ`et]

▶ (動詞) 創造，創作

【三態：create/created/created】

🔊 Andy likes to create songs.
安迪喜歡創作歌曲。

•6. presentation [ˌprizɛn`teʃən]

▶ (名詞) 顯示，呈現

🔊 It takes practice to give a good teaching presentation.
好的教學呈現需要練習。

•7. professional [prə`fɛʃən!]

▶ (形容詞) 專業的

🔊 Luna is a professional dancer.
露娜是專業的舞者。

•8. pianist [pɪ`ænɪst]

▶ (名詞) 鋼琴家

🔊 It takes practice to be a good pianist.
要成為好的鋼琴家需要練習。

•9. concert [`kansɚt]

▶ (名詞) 音樂會，演奏會

🔊 Angela came to Taipei to hear a concert.
安琪拉來台北聽音樂會。

● 工作場合
❷ 學習場合
❸ 朋友場合

5. 學習心得
(learning experiences)

相關用語

1. It is fun and easy to learn how to sing.
   學習如何唱歌是有趣跟容易的。

2. Excel is a really convenient program for calculations.
   Excel真是計算上一個很方便的軟體。

3. This painting class has helped me to let go of myself.
   這門繪畫課已幫助我釋放自己。

4. I really like the warm atmosphere in the small class.
   我真的好喜歡這小班級裡溫馨的氣氛。

5. Dancing is a good way to make new friends.
   跳舞是認識新朋友的好方法。

6. I am so happy that I can cook well now.
   真的好高興我現在很會做菜。

單字、片語、句型解說

● 1. fun [fʌn]

▶ (形容詞) 有趣的

例 I had a fun night out.
我在外面度過了一個有趣的夜晚。

● 2. Excel [ɪk`sɛl]

▶ (名詞) 微軟公司的試算表軟體

例 Can you teach me to use Excel?
你可以教我使用Excel嗎？

● 3. convenient [kən`vinjənt]

▶ (形容詞) 方便的

例 Is this time convenient for you?
這個時間你方便嗎？

● 4. program [`progræm]

▶ (名詞) 程式，軟體

例 You can download this program for free.
你可以免費下載這個軟體。

● 5. calculation [ˌkælkjə`leʃən]

▶ (名詞) 計算

① 工作場合
② 學習場合
③ 朋友場合

例 Your calculation is right.
你的計算是正確的。

●6. painting [`pentɪŋ]

▶ (形容詞) 繪畫的

例 I really like her painting style.
我真的很喜歡她的繪畫風格。

●7. let go of [lɛt] [go] [ɑv]

▶ (動詞片語) 釋放…，放開…

例 Let go of the past!
放下過去吧！

●8. warm [wɔrm]

▶ (形容詞) 溫馨的，溫暖的

例 I like her warm smile.
我喜歡她溫暖的笑容。

●9. cook [kʊk]

▶ (動詞) 煮，烹調

【三態：cook/cooked/cooked】

例 Can you cook well?
你很會做菜嗎？

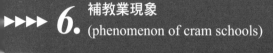

▶▶▶▶ **6.** 補教業現象
(phenomenon of cram schools)

相關用語

1. In Taiwan, you can see cram schools everywhere.
   補習班在台灣隨處可見。

2. Cram schools are many peoples' memory about high school period.
   補習班是許多人中學時期的回憶。

3. Cram schools may never disappear because of competition.
   由於競爭之故，補習班也許永遠不會消失。

4. Many students attend cram schools to improve their scores on the entrance exams.
   許多學生上補習班是為了改善升學考試的成績。

5. Educational reform aims to reduce the need for cram schooling.
   教育改革旨在降低對補習的需求。

單字、片語、句型解說

● 1. everywhere [ˋɛvrɪˏhwɛr]

▶ (副詞) 到處

例 There are people everywhere in the market.

市場裡到處都是人。

● 2. memory [ˋmɛmərɪ]

▶ (名詞) 記憶

例 I have a poor memory for names.

我對名字的記性很差。

● 3. period [ˋpɪrɪəd]

▶ (名詞) 時期

例 This was the happiest period of my life.

這是我一生中最快樂的時期。

● 4. disappear [ˏdɪsəˋpɪr]

▶ (動詞) 消失

【三態：disappear/disappeared/disappeared】

例 What will make love disappear?

什麼東西會讓愛消失？

083

5. because of [bɪ`kɔz] [ɑv]+名詞/動名詞

▶【因為…】

例 I didn't go to school because of a cold.
因為感冒,所以我沒有去學校。

6. competition [ˌkɑmpə`tɪʃən]

▶ (名詞) 競爭

例 Maybe competition among students is good.
也許學生之間有競爭是好的。

7. attend [ə`tɛnd]

▶ (動詞) 上學,上課

【三態:attend/attended/attended】

例 He didn't attend the class yesterday.
他昨天沒有來上課。

8. score [skor]

▶ (名詞) 分數,成績

例 I got a high score on the test.
我測驗得了高分。

9. the entrance exams [ði] [`ɛntrəns] [ɪg`zæmz]

▶ (名詞片語) 入學考試

① 工作場合
② 學習場合
③ 朋友場合

例 The competition of the entrance
exams in Taiwan is very keen.
台灣升學考試的競爭非常激烈。

● 10. educational [ˌɛdʒʊˈkeʃən!]

▶ (形容詞) 教育的

例 I will attend an educational meeting
next Friday.
下週五我會出席一場教育會議。

● 11. reform [rɪˈfɔrm]

▶ (名詞) 改革

例 Educational reforms are needed in
this country.
這個國家需要教育改革。

● 12. aim to [em] [tu]+V

▶ 【意欲…，旨在…】

例 This class aims to improve computer
skills.
這門課旨在改善電腦技能。

● 13. reduce [rɪˈdjus]

▶ (動詞) 減少，降低

【三態：reduce/reduced/reduced】

例 My company is trying to reduce costs.
我的公司正設法降低成本。

Chapter

3

朋友場合
(Being with Friends)

Lesson 1
聚餐
(Dining Together)

　　中國人是個對飲食文化極為講究的民族，不論是同事聚會、公司尾牙、家庭聚餐、生日慶祝、同學會、慶功宴等等，總喜歡聚在一起聊天說地、享受美食，如果受邀名單之中有國外的友人，那麼不論是在時間地點的通知、聚餐的原因，以及餐點及聚餐活動的介紹上，如果知道如何運用適當的英文與之溝通，將會使聚餐活動更為愉快，也增進了與國外朋友的友誼！

❶ 工作場合　❷ 學習場合　**❸ 朋友場合**

引言的關鍵單字或片語：

1. dine [daɪn]　　　　　　(動詞)用餐，吃飯

2. an annual dinner [æn] [`ænjʊəl] [`dɪnɚ]
　　　　　　　　　　　　(名詞片語)尾牙

3. a class reunion [ə] [klæs] [ri`junjən]
　　　　　　　　　　　　(名詞片語)同學會

4. a celebration party [ə] [ˌsɛlə`breʃən] [`pɑrtɪ]
　　　　　　　　　　　　(名詞片語)慶功宴

5. reason [`rizən]　　　　(名詞)理由

6. activity [æk`tɪvətɪ]　　(名詞)活動

MP3 085

1. 聚餐原因
(reasons for dining together)

相關用語

1. We hold this dinner party to celebrate Mother's Day.
   我們舉辦晚宴來慶祝母親節。

2. My company will have a celebration party because we reached our sales target.
   因為我們達到業績，公司將舉行慶功宴。

3. This is our first class reunion after graduation.
   這是我們畢業後第一次的同學會。

4. I'd like to treat both of you to dinner after class.
   下課後我想請你們兩個人吃晚餐。

5. We plan to throw a party at our house to celebrate Annie's birthday.
   我們打算在家裡舉行派對來慶祝安妮的生日。

單字、片語、句型解說

● 1. celebrate [ˋsɛləˌbret]

▶ (動詞) 慶祝

【三態：celebrate/celebrated/celebrated】

例 We held a party to celebrate Andy's birthday.

我們舉行宴會慶祝安迪的生日。

> celebration [ˌsɛləˋbreʃən]
> (名詞) 慶祝

> a celebration party
> (名詞片語) 慶功宴

【補充】an annual dinner [æn] [ˋænjʊəl] [ˋdɪnɚ]

(名詞片語) 尾牙

例 Where will your company hold the annual dinner?

你們公司將在哪裡辦尾牙？

● 2. reach [ritʃ]

▶ (動詞) 達到 【三態：reach/reached/reached】

例 When will we reach Taipei?

我們什麼時候會到台北？

MP3 086

●3. sales [selz]

▶ (形容詞) 銷售的

例 His girlfriend is a sales clerk.
他的女友是一個銷售員。

●4. target [`tɑrgɪt]

▶ (名詞) 目標

例 We work hard to reach the targets.
我們努力工作以期達成目標。

●5. reunion [ri`junjən]

▶ (名詞) 團聚

例 Our family reunion is very important to us.
我們的家庭聚會對我們來說非常重要。

●6. graduation [,grædʒʊ`eʃən]

▶ (名詞) 畢業

例 My parents hope that I can get a good job after graduation.
爸媽希望我畢業後可以找到好工作。

●7. treat [trit]+人+to [tu]+東西

▶ 【招待…人…東西】

例 Thank you for treating me to dinner.
謝謝你請我吃晚餐。

●8. plan [plæn]+to V

▶ 【計劃去…，打算去…】

例 What do you plan to do after graduation?
畢業後你打算做什麼？

●9. throw [θro]

▶ (動詞) (口語常用) 舉行 (宴會等)

【三態：throw/threw/thrown】

例 We threw a party for our boss last night.
昨晚我們替老闆舉行了派對。

●10.【補充】常見的聚餐原因：

▶ (1)birthday (生日)

(2)family reunion (家庭聚會)

(3)class reunion (同學會)

(4)an annual dinner (尾牙)

(5)a celebration party (慶功宴)

(6)holidays and festivals (假日與節慶)

① 工作場合
② 學習場合
③ 朋友場合

2. 時間、地點
(time & place)

相關用語

1. Would you like to have dinner with us tonight?
   你今天晚上想和我們一起用餐嗎？

2. My family plan to have a barbebue at home on the Moon Festival.
   我家人計劃在中秋節時在家裡烤肉。

3. We are having a birthday party for Kelly at an all-you-can-eat restaurant.
   我們將在一家吃到飽的餐廳為凱莉慶祝生日。

4. Our 5th class reunion is to be held on September 8 at the Grand Hotel.
   我們第五屆的同學會將於九月八日於圓山大飯店舉行。

5. My company's annual dinner is to be held at a famous hotel.
   我們公司的尾牙將在一間著名的飯店舉行。

單字、片語、句型解說

● 1. barbecue [`bɑrbɪkju]

► (名詞) 烤肉

例 Will you have a barbecue on the Moon Festival?
你們中秋節時會烤肉嗎？

● 2. the Moon Festival [ðə] [mun] [`fɛstəvḷ]

► (名詞片語) 中秋節

● 3. all-you-can-eat [ɔl] [ju] [kæn] [it]

► (形容詞) 吃到飽的

例 I want to treat you to an all-you-can-eat buffet at that restaurant.
我想請你去那家餐廳享用吃到飽的自助餐。

● 4. is to be held

► 這邊有表「未來」的意味，意思為「將被舉行」。

be動詞+to be pp(過去分詞)→為表未來的被動式，(動詞)「舉行」的三態為「hold/held/held」。

● 5. the Grand Hotel [ðə] [grænd] [ho`tɛl]

► (名詞片語) 圓山大飯店

3. 餐點、活動
(meals & activities)

相關用語

1. I will perform dancing during the company's annual dinner.
   我將在尾牙中表演跳舞。

2. They will buy me a cake and some wine to celebrate my birthday.
   他們會買蛋糕跟一點酒來慶祝我的生日。

3. There will be pizzas, snacks and beverages in the celebration party.
   慶功宴上將有披薩、點心和飲料。

4. We will invite a live band and DJ for the guests on that day.
   那一天我們會替賓客們請來現場樂團及唱片騎師。

5. Let's go to that Indian restaurant to enjoy some curry dishes.
   我們去那一家印度餐廳享用一些咖哩菜餚吧。

6. A famous female singer will perform her greatest hits at the dinner party.
   一位著名的女歌手將在晚宴上表演她的成名曲。

單字、片語、句型解說

●1. snack [snæk]

▶ (名詞) 點心，小吃

例 I feel you will like the snacks in the night market.
我覺得你會喜歡夜市裡的小吃。

●2. beverage [`bɛvərɪdʒ]

▶ (名詞) 飲料

例 We can't have any beverages in class.
我們在上課中不能喝任何飲料。

●3. invite [ɪn`vaɪt]

▶ (動詞) 邀請 【三態：invite/invited/invited】

例 I will invite all of my classmates to the party.
我會邀請所有的同學來參加派對。

●4. a live band [ə] [laɪv] [bænd]

▶ (名詞片語) 現場演出的樂團

例 I plan to invite a live band to the party.
我打算要請一個樂團在宴會上現場表演。

●5. guest [gɛst]

▶ (名詞) 客人，賓客

例 Mr. Ho is our important guest.
何先生是我們重要的客人。

●6. Indian [ˋɪndɪən]

▶ (形容詞) 印度的

例 I am interested in Indian music.
我對印度音樂感興趣。

●7. curry [ˋkɝɪ]

▶ (名詞) 咖哩

例 I like to eat curry chicken rice.
我喜歡吃咖哩雞飯。

●8. female [ˋfimel]

▶ (形容詞) 女性的

例 There are 25 female students in our class.
我們班有二十五個女學生。

●9. the greatest hit [ðə] [ˋgretɪst] [hɪt]

▶ (名詞片語) 成名曲

例 What are Jay Chou's greatest hits?
周杰倫的成名曲有哪些？

Lesson 2
文化娛樂活動
(Cultural & Recreational Activities)

　　現代人普遍步調緊張，工作壓力大，常常需要在工作與休閒之間取得平衡。因而閒暇之餘參與文化娛樂活動，諸如音樂會、逛書展、欣賞電影等等，不但能紓解壓力，也能滿足精神上的需求，賦予生活教育及啟發意義。而不論是表演的音樂家、藝人，抑或是現場提供的資料等等，都可能以英文來呈現內容及精神。如果能熟悉這樣場合裡的英文常用語，就能與國外的友人達到好的精神文化交流。

① 工作場合

② 學習場合

③ 朋友場合

引言的關鍵單字或片語：

1. cultural [`kʌltʃərəl]　　　(形容詞)文化的

2. recreational [ˌrɛkrɪ`eʃən!]
　　　　　　　(形容詞)消遣的，娛樂的

3. pressure [`prɛʃər]　　　(名詞)壓力

4. leisure time [`liʒər] [taɪm]
　　　　　　　　(名詞片語)休閒

5. balance [`bæləns]　　　(名詞)平衡

6. concert [ˈkɑnsɚt]　　(名詞)音樂會，演奏會

7. exhibition [ˌɛksəˈbɪʃən](名詞)展覽

8. enlightenment [ɪnˈlaɪtənmənt]
　　　　　　　　　　(名詞)啟發

9. musician [mjuˈzɪʃən]　(名詞)音樂家

10. artist [ˈɑrtɪst]　　　(名詞)藝術家，藝人

11. content [ˈkɑntɛnt]　(名詞)內容

12. spirit [ˈspɪrɪt]　　　(名詞)精神

▶▶▶▶ 1. 音樂會、演唱會 (concerts)

相關用語

1. Today's concert features traditional Chinese music.
   今天的音樂會以傳統國樂為特色。

2. Since 1983, this excellent cellist has performed many solo concerts.
   自從 1983 年以來，這位優秀的大提琴家已經舉辦過多場的獨奏會。

3. How did you like today's concert?
   今天的音樂會(演唱會)你還喜歡嗎？

4. I like Aaron Kwo's performance; he dances so well!
   我喜歡郭富城的表演，他好會跳舞喔！

5. Leehom Wang's slow songs are full of emotions.
   王力宏的慢歌感情豐富。

6. Let's clap and scream for an encore.
   我們一起來拍手喊安可吧。

③ 朋友場合

單字、片語、句型解說

● 1. feature [fitʃɚ]

▶ (動詞) 以⋯為特色

【三態：feature/featured/featured】

例 The museum features paintings.

這間博物館以展出繪畫為特色。

● 2. traditional [trə`dɪʃən!]

▶ (形容詞) 傳統的

例 I enjoy listening to traditional Chinese music.

我喜歡聽國樂。

● 3. since+過去時間,句子(要用現在完成式：have/has+pp).

▶ since [sɪns] (介係詞) 自從⋯

例 I haven't met him since last year.

從去年以來我就沒有遇見過他。

● 4. cellist [`tʃɛlɪst]

▶ (名詞) 大提琴家

例 Yo-yo Ma is a great cellist.

馬友友是一個偉大的大提琴家。

092

●5. be 動詞+full of [fʊl] [ɑv]+名詞

► 【充滿了…】

例 The bus is full of people.
公車上都是人。

●6. emotion [ɪˋmoʃən]

► (名詞) 感情，情感

例 She sings with emotion.
她用感情唱歌。

●7. clap [klæp]

► (動詞) 拍手【三態：clap/clapped/clapped】

例 We clapped for the cellist.
我們替大提琴家鼓掌。

●8. scream [skrim]

► (動詞) 尖叫

【三態：scream/screamed/screamed】

例 The fans screamed when they saw the movie star.
看到那位電影明星，影迷們尖叫。

3 朋友場合

2. 展覽
(exhibitions)

相關用語

1. The book fair will be held at the Taipei World Trade Center.
   這個書展將於台北世界貿易中心舉行。

2. The exhibition is a diverse international computer fair.
   這個展覽是一個多元的國際電腦展。

3. This exhibition features selections of Chinese calligraphy.
   這個展覽以中國書法的選集為特色。

4. The exhibition will consist of works of the well-known modern artist.
   這個展覽將展出這個著名當代藝術家的作品。

093

單字、片語、句型解說

1. fair [fɛr]

▶ (名詞) 商品展覽會,博覽會

例 A computer fair is to be held next week.

下星期將舉辦電腦展。

2. the Taipei World Trade Center [ðə] [ˋtaɪˋpe] [wɝˋld] [tred] [ˋsɛntɚ]

▶ (名詞片語) 台北世界貿易中心

3. diverse [daɪˋvɝs]

▶ (形容詞) 多樣的,多元的

例 Students have diverse talents.

學生們有不同的天賦。

4. international [ˌɪntɚˋnæʃənḷ]

▶ (形容詞) 國際(性)的

例 This is an international book fair.

這是一個國際性的書展。

5. selection [səˋlɛkʃən]

▶ (名詞) 選集,被挑選出的人或物

❸ 朋友場合

197

例 This book consists of selections of my works.

這本書包含了我的作品選集。

●6. consist of [kən`sɪst] [ɑv]

▶ (動詞片語) 由…所組成

例 Our class consists of 35 students.

我們班由三十五個學生所組成。

●7. work [wɝk]

▶ (名詞) 作品

例 I like the artist's early works.

我喜歡這個藝術家早期的作品。

●8. well-known [`wɛl`non]

▶ (形容詞) 著名的，眾所周知

例 Andy Liu is a well-known actor.

劉德華是一個著名的演員。

●9. artist [`ɑrtɪst]

▶ (名詞) 藝術家，美術家

●art [ɑrt]

▶ (名詞)藝術，美術

例 The artist teaches art history.

這位藝術家教授藝術史。

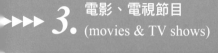

3. 電影、電視節目 (movies & TV shows)

相關用語

1. I'd like to go to see the movie, "The Fierce Wife."
   我想去看「犀利人妻」這部電影。

2. I heard this movie is playing at the movie theater.
   我聽說這部電影正在上映中。

3. I like to have popcorn and hot dogs at the theater.
   我喜歡在電影院吃爆米花和熱狗。

4. The movie will last for about 3 hours.
   這部電影大概長達三個小時。

5. Maggie, did you see the news today?
   梅姬,你今天看過新聞了嗎?

6. What's on channel 11 at 9:00?
   九點時第十一頻道是什麼節目?

7. Do you like to watch soap operas?
   你喜歡看連續劇嗎?

❸ 朋友場合

單字、片語、句型解說

1. fierce [fɪrs]

(形容詞) 兇猛的，好鬥的

例 This dog is very fierce.
這隻狗好兇。

2. play [ple]

(動詞) 上演，表演

【三態：play/played/played】

例 When will the movie play in Taipei?
這部電影台北何時上映？

3. a movie theater [ə] [`muvɪ] [`θɪətə]

(名詞片語) 戲院

例 Where is the nearest movie theater?
最近的一家電影院在哪裡？

4. popcorn [`pɑp,kɔrn]

(名詞) 爆玉米花

例 I will buy popcorn at the movie
theater.
我會在電影院買爆玉米花。

5. hot dogs [hɑt] [dɔgz]

(名詞片語) 熱狗

例 Does McDonald's sell hot dogs?
麥當勞有賣熱狗嗎?

 095

●6. about [ə`baʊt]

▶ (介係詞) 大約，大概

例 I will reach Taipei about 3 o'clock in the afternoon.
我大概在下午三點會到台北。

●7. channel [`tʃæn!]

▶ (名詞) 頻道

例 How many television channels are there in Taiwan?
台灣有多少個電視頻道?

●8. a soap opera [ə] [sop] [`ɑpərə]

▶ (名詞片語) 連續劇

例 I like to watch soap operas on TV.
我喜歡看電視連續劇。

電影類型

中文	對應之英文	英文音標
動作片	an action film	[æn] [ˋækʃən] [fɪlm]
動畫片／卡通片	an animation	[æn] [ˏænəˋmeʃən]
災難片	a disaster film	[ə] [dɪˋzæstɚ] [fɪlm]
恐怖片	a horror film	[ə] [ˋhɔrɚ] [fɪlm]
愛情片	a romance	[ə] [roˋmæns]
科幻片	a sci-fi film	[ə] [ˋsaɪˋfaɪ] [fɪlm]
驚悚片	a thriller	[ə] [ˋθrɪlɚ]
戰爭片	a war film	[ə] [wɔr] [fɪlm]

096

電視類型

中文	對應之英文	英文音標
綜藝節目	a variety show	[ə] [vəˋraɪətɪ] [ʃo]
連續劇	a soap opera	[ə] [sop] [ˋɑpərə]
談話性節目	a talk show	[ə] [tɔk] [ʃo]
新聞節目	a news program	[ə] [njuz] [ˋprogræm]
紀錄片節目	a documentary program	[ə] [ˌdɑkjəˋmɛntərɪ] [ˋprogræm]
兒童卡通節目	a children's cartoon program	[ə] [ˋtʃɪldrənz] [karˋtun] [ˋprogræm]
教育性節目	an educational TV program	[æn] [ˌɛdʒʊˋkeʃən!] [ˋtiˋvi]

朋友場合

MP3 097

Lesson 3

體育活動
(Sports Activities)

　　台灣有許多盛行的體育活動，例如台灣的職業棒球比賽，往往吸引滿坑滿谷的觀眾。場內緊張的比賽，緊扣著球迷的心弦，而場外攤販的叫賣，也是十分熱鬧，共同形塑台灣特有的棒球文化。而在國外，運動也是非常風行，像是美國的美式足球、NBA籃球等等。運動不但健身，也為生活帶來許多樂趣和話題。如果能夠和國外的友人聊運動、分享運動的樂趣，一定會更增進彼此的情誼。

引言的關鍵單字或片語：

1. a sports activity [ə] [spɔrts] [æk`tɪvətɪ]
   (名詞片語)體育活動

2. a baseball game [ə] [`bes,bɔl] [gem]
   (名詞片語)棒球比賽

3. audience [`ɔdɪəns]　　(名詞)觀眾

4. fan [fæn]　　(名詞)球迷

5. vendor [`vɛndɚ]　　(名詞)小販

6. football [`fʊt,bɔl]　　(名詞)美式足球

7. basketball [`bæskɪtˌbɔl] (名詞)籃球

8. pleasure [`plɛʒɚ] (名詞)樂趣

9. topic [`tɑpɪk] (名詞)話題

10. share [ʃɛr] (動詞)分享

MP3 098

1. 聊運動
(talking about exercise & sports)

相關用語

1. I'd like to exercise.
   我想去運動。

2. Let's go to the gym.
   我們去體育館吧。

3. I like to play basketball.
   我喜歡打籃球。

4. What exercises do you usually do?
   你平常做什麼運動？

5. How well do you play tennis?
   你網球打得怎麼樣？

6. Maybe we can play soccer together at the stadium.
   也許我們可以一起去運動場踢足球。

7. I think volleyball is an interesting sport.
   我覺得排球是一項有趣的運動。

單字、片語、句型解說

●1. exercise [ˋɛksəˏsaɪz]

▶ (動詞／名詞) 運動

【三態：exercise/exercised/exercised】

例 How often do you exercise?
你多常運動？

●2. gym [dʒɪm]

▶ (名詞) 體育館

例 Are you often at the gym?
你常在體育館裡嗎？

●3. tennis [ˋtɛnɪs]

▶ (名詞) 網球

例 They often play tennis in the park.
他們常在公園裡打網球。

●4. soccer [ˋsɑkə]

▶ (名詞) 足球

例 Do you like to play soccer?
你喜歡踢足球嗎？

❸ 朋友場合

MP3 099

•5. stadium [`stedɪəm]

► (名詞) 體育場，運動場

例 I will go to the stadium to watch the baseball game.
我會去體育場看棒球賽。

•6. volleyball [`vɑlɪˌbɔl]

► (名詞) 排球

例 Where can we play volleyball in Taipei?
台北哪裡可以打排球？

•7. interesting [`ɪntərɪstɪŋ]

► (形容詞) 有趣的

例 Is this book interesting?
這本書有趣嗎？

•8. sport [sport]

► (名詞) 運動

例 What sports do you play?
你做什麼運動？

2. 聊運動比賽
(talking about sports)

相關用語

1. It's wonderful to watch baseball games at a stadium.
   在運動場看棒球賽很棒。

2. Do you like to watch SBL basketball games?
   你喜歡看台灣超級籃球聯賽的籃球比賽嗎？

3. I have been watching the NBA for many years.
   我看NBA美國職業籃球已經很多年了。

4. I've been shouting and cheering while watching the World Cup.
   在看世界盃足球賽時，我一直在喊加油。

5. Can you find a bar that broadcasts American football games?
   你可以找到播放美式足球比賽的酒吧嗎？

6. I like to watch both CPBL and MLB baseball games.
   中華職棒跟美國職棒大聯盟的比賽我都喜歡看。

❸ 朋友場合

單字、片語、句型解說

● 1. wonderful [`wʌndɚfəl]

▶ (形容詞) 極好的

例 This is a wonderful song.
這首歌好棒。

● 2. baseball [`besˌbɔl]

▶ (名詞) 棒球

例 Baseball is very popular in Taiwan.
棒球在台灣很受歡迎。

● 3. SBL 為「Super Basketball League」的縮寫

▶ 意思為「超級籃球聯賽」。

● 4. have been+V-ing(watching)

▶「現在完成進行式」。

● 5. NBA 為「National Basketball Association」的縮寫

▶ 意思為「美國國家職業籃球協會」。

● 6. shout [ʃaʊt]

▶ (動詞) 呼喊，喊叫

【三態：shout/shouted/shouted】

例 Don't shout at me.
別對我大喊大叫。

●7. cheer [tʃɪr]

> (動詞) 歡呼，喝采

【三態：cheer/cheered/cheered】

例 They cheered when we kissed.
當我們接吻時，他們歡呼了起來。

●8. while [hwaɪ]

> (副詞連接詞) 正當

例 I kissed her while she was sleeping.
正當她在睡覺的時候，我吻了她。

●9. the World Cup [ðə] [wɜˈld] [kʌp]

> (名詞片語) 世界盃足球賽

●10. broadcast [`brɔd,kæst]

> (動詞) 廣播，播送 【三態同形】

例 The World Cup will be broadcast on television.
世界盃足球賽將進行電視轉播。

●11. football [`fʊt,bɔl]

> (名詞) 美式足球

●12. 台灣人對棒球非常的狂熱，常見的職業棒球討論話題為：

> 「CPBL中華職業棒球大聯盟（Chinese Professional Baseball League）」以及「MLB美國職棒大聯盟（Major League Baseball）」。

3 朋友場合

MP3 101

Lesson4
聊興趣、嗜好
(Interests & Hobbies)

興趣或嗜好通常都是朋友聚在一起時的好話題，有相同興趣或嗜好的人也通常較能成為好朋友。

每個人的興趣或嗜好其實也多少反映出每個人的個性，好動的人通常坐不住，喜歡戶外活動或是運動；愛美的人通常會注意時尚訊息，喜歡逛街、研究流行衣物等等；安靜的人則會選擇看書、聽音樂、或是在家上網做宅男宅女。

引言的關鍵單字或片語：

1. interest [ˈɪntərɪst]　　　　(名詞)興趣

2. hobby [ˈhɑbɪ]　　　　(名詞)嗜好

3. personality
[ˌpɝsənˈælətɪ]　　　　(名詞)個性

4. an outdoor activity [æn] [ˈaʊtˌdor]
[ækˈtɪvətɪ]　　　　(名詞片語)戶外活動

5. fashion [ˈfæʃən]　　　(名詞)流行式樣，時尚

6. an indoor activity [æn] [ˈɪnˌdor] [ækˈtɪvətɪ]
　　　　　　　　(名詞片語)戶內活動

▶▶▶▶ 1. 靜態 (sedentary activities)

相關用語

1. What kind of music do you usually listen to?
   通常你都聽什麼樣的音樂？

2. Pop is my favorite kind of music.
   流行音樂是我最喜歡的音樂類型。

3. I would like to join a book club.
   我想要加入讀書會。

4. The book I am reading is about a famous singer.
   我正在讀的這本書內容是關於一位著名的歌手。

5. Would you like to go to the library with me?
   你想要和我一起去圖書館嗎？

6. I am addicted to the Internet.
   我沉迷於網路。

❸ 朋友場合

單字、片語、句型解說

● 1. kind [kaɪnd]

▶ (名詞) 種類

例 What kind of books do you usually read?
你通常閱讀什麼樣的書？

● 2. listen [`lɪsən]

▶ (動詞) 聽 【三態：listen/listened/listened】

例 Please listen to me.
請聽我說。

● 3. pop [pɑp]

▶ (名詞) 流行音樂

例 I like to listen to pop.
我喜歡聽流行音樂。

● 4. join [dʒɔɪn]

▶ (動詞) 加入 【三態：join/joined/joined】

例 Will you join our club?
你會加入我們的俱樂部嗎？

● 5. club [klʌb]

▶ 俱樂部，社團

例 What club do you want to join?
你想要加入什麼社團？

103

●6. addict [əˋdɪkt]

► (動詞) 沉迷，上癮

【三態：addict/addicted/addicted】

例 Don't be addicted to television.
不要沉迷於電視。

●7. Internet [ˋɪntɚ͵nɛt]

► (名詞) 網路

例 Many students are addicted to the Internet.
很多學生沉迷於網路。

●8.【補充】常見的靜態活動：

► (1)listening to music (聽音樂)

(2)reading books (看書)

(3)playing on the computer (玩電腦)

(4)playing musical instruments (玩樂器)

(5)watching TV (看電視)

(6)planting flowers (種花)

(7)surfing the Internet (上網)

❸ 朋友場合

2. 動態
(dynamic activities)

相關用語

1. I like to go on a trip with my family.
   我喜歡跟家人一起去旅遊。

2. I like to play basketball in the school gym on weekends.
   我喜歡周末時在學校的體育館裡打籃球。

3. What's your favorite sport?
   你最喜歡的運動是什麼？

4. What kind of outdoor activities do you enjoy?
   你喜歡什麼樣的戶外活動？

5. I like camping the most.
   我最喜歡露營了。

6. I love to play with the kids at the park.
   我喜歡跟小孩子們在公園玩。

7. I often go biking with my friends on Sundays.
   我常在周日時跟我的朋友去騎腳踏車。

104

單字、片語、句型解說

●1. go on a trip [go] [ɑn] [ə] [trɪp]

▶ (動詞片語) 去旅行

> trip [trɪp]
> (名詞) 旅行

例 I plan to go on a trip with my best friend.
我打算和最好的朋友去旅行。

●2. outdoor [ˈaʊtˌdor]

▶ (形容詞) 戶外的

例 Do you like outdoor sports?
你喜歡戶外運動嗎？

●3. camping [ˈkæmpɪŋ]

▶ (動名詞) 露營

例 We will go camping this Sunday.
這週日我們將去露營。

●4. the most [ðə] [most]

▶ (副詞最高級) 最…

例 I like to play basketball the most.
我最喜歡打籃球了。

❸ 朋友場合

●5. kid [kɪd]

▶ (名詞) (口語) 小孩

例 Do you like kids?
你喜歡小孩嗎?

●6. bike [baɪk]

▶ (動詞) (口語) 騎腳踏車

【三態:bike/biked/biked】

go+V-ing
【表從事…活動】

例 I want to go biking with my boyfriend.
我想要跟男朋友去騎單車。

●7. on Sundays [ɑn] [`sʌndez]

▶ (=every Sunday) 每逢星期天

例 We often go shopping on Sundays.
我們常在週日去購物。

Lesson 5

聊近況
(Talking About Recent Situations)

　　朋友間總是需要彼此分享近況,一方面可以紓壓,一方面可以提供建議和關心。而不論是快樂或悲傷的消息,如果可以跟朋友分享,也許將可以使快樂加倍、悲傷減半。

　　所以不論在下班後或是在假日,和朋友聚餐或是一起活動時,別忘了適時地表達對朋友的關心,也許朋友需要你給予工作上的建議,也許朋友的家人最近有新的動向,也許朋友在感情上受到打擊,也許朋友身體微恙健康不佳。此時積極地伸出友誼的手,去傾聽、去分享、去付出,將使友情散發溫馨的芬芳。

引言的關鍵單字或片語:

1. recent [`risənt]　　　　　(形容詞)最近的

2. situation [ˌsɪtʃʊ`eʃən] (名詞)情況,處境

3. suggestion [sə`dʒɛstʃən]　(名詞)建議

4. care [kɛr]　　　　　(名詞)關心

5. happiness [`hæpɪnɪs] (名詞)快樂

3 朋友場合

6. sadness [`sædnɪs]　　　(名詞)悲傷

7. development [dɪ`vɛləpmənt]
　　　　　　　　　(名詞)事態發展，新動向

8. frustration [ˌfrʌs`treʃən]　　(名詞)挫折

9. indisposition [ˌɪndɪspə`zɪʃən]
　　　　　　　　　(名詞)不舒服，微恙

10. friendship [`frɛndʃɪp]　(名詞)友誼

106

▶▶▶ *1.* 工作 (work)

相關用語

1. How have you been?
   你最近怎麼樣？

2. Where are you working now?
   你現在在哪裡上班？

3. Did you hear that John got fired last month?
   約翰上個月被炒魷魚，你聽說了嗎？

4. There's a job opening at my company this week.
   這周我們公司有招聘會。

5. I need to find a new job.
   我需要找一份新的工作。

6. I will have an interview this Friday.
   這周五我將有一個面試。

7. I feel stressed out with my work.
   我工作壓力真的好大。

❸ 朋友場合

單字、片語、句型解說

●1. have been 是「have+pp」，為現在

> ▶

be動詞的三態是：be/was,were/been

●2. hear [hɪr]

> ▶ (動詞) 聽說 【三態：hear/heard/heard】

例 I heard that she moved to Taipei last month.

我聽說她上個月搬到台北了。

●3. fire [faɪr]

> ▶ (動詞) (口語) 解雇，開除

【三態：fire/fired/fired】

get [gɛt]的三態為get/got/got,gotten，這邊用的是過去式got

get+fired，為get+pp，表「變成…狀態」。

●4. opening [`opənɪŋ]

> ▶ (名詞) (職位的) 空缺

例 Are there openings in your company?

你們公司有缺人嗎？

107

●5. interview [ˋɪntɚˏvju]

▶ (名詞) 面試

例 He was late for the interview, so he didn't get the job.
他面試遲到了，所以沒有被錄取。

●6. stressed out [strɛst] [aʊt]

▶ (形容詞片語) 緊張的，感到有壓力的

例 Are you stressed out after work every day?
你每天下班後都疲憊不堪嗎？

●7.【補充】常見的職稱：

▶ (1)teacher (老師)
(2)clerk (職員)
(3)secretary (秘書)
(4)doctor (醫生)
(5)salesman (業務員)
(6)civil servant (公務員)

❸ 朋友場合

▶▶▶▶▶ ## 2. 家人 (family)

相關用語

1. How's your family?
   你的家人好嗎？

2. Is your son in America now?
   你的兒子現在在美國嗎？

3. My husband is in Shanghai with our kids.
   我的先生和孩子們在上海。

4. Please tell your wife I said hi.
   請代我向你妻子問好。

5. I'm really worried that my daughter might get laid off.
   我真的很擔心我的女兒會被裁員。

6. My mother-in-law often comes over for lunch on Saturdays.
   我岳母周六時常過來家裡吃午餐。

7. We like to cook and dine at home.
   我們喜歡在家煮飯用餐。

單字、片語、句型解說

●1. son [sʌn]

► (名詞) 兒子

例 How many sons do you have?
你有幾個兒子？

●2. husband [ˋhʌzbənd]

► (名詞) 先生，丈夫

例 I met your husband at the park last night.
昨晚我在公園遇到妳先生。

●3. tell [tɛl]

► (動詞) 告訴 【三態：tell/told/told】

例 Can you tell me your phone number?
可以告訴我你的電話號碼嗎？

●4. worried [ˋwɝɪd]

► (形容詞) 擔心的

例 What are you worried about?
你在擔心什麼？

❸ 朋友場合

●5. lay off [le] [ɔf]

▶ (動詞片語) 解雇 【三態：lay/laid/laid】
get laid為get+pp(laid)，有「變成…狀態」之意。

例 My company laid off 10 workers last year.
去年我公司解雇了十名工人。

●6. mother-in-law [ˋmʌðərɪnˏlɔ]

▶ (名詞) 婆婆，岳母

例 My mother-in-law often babysits for us.
我的岳母常常幫我們照顧小孩。

●7. come over [kʌm] [ˋovɚ]

▶ (動詞片語) 從遠方過來，順便來訪

例 Please come over any time.
請隨時都可以過來坐坐。

●8. dine [daɪn]

▶ (動詞) 用餐 【三態：dine/dined/dined】

例 I will dine with my daughter tonight.
今晚我將和我的女兒一起用餐。

3. 感情
(love relationships)

相關用語

1. What's bothering you?
   怎麼啦？

2. I broke up with my boyfriend and I feel really sad.
   我跟男友分手了，我覺得好難過。

3. I hope you feel better soon.
   我希望你很快好起來。

4. My wife got pregnant two weeks ago.
   我的老婆兩周前懷孕了。

5. Maybe we will get married next year.
   也許我們明年會結婚。

6. I am single and feel lonely.
   我單身，感到寂寞。

7. I'd like to introduce a girl to you.
   我想要介紹一個女孩給你認識。

❸ 朋友場合

單字、片語、句型解說

●1. bother [`baðɚ]

▶ (動詞) 打擾，困擾

【三態：bother/bothered/bothered】

例 Don't bother me!
不要煩我！

●2. break up with [brek] [ʌp] [wɪð]+人

▶ 【跟…分手】

> break [brek]
> (動詞) 打破，中止

【三態：break/broke/broken】

●3. feel [fil]+形容詞(比較級)

▶ 【覺得…】

例 I feel happy for you.
我替你感到高興。

●4. sad [sæd]

▶ (形容詞) 傷心的，難過的

例 Why are you so sad?
你為什麼這麼難過？

●5. pregnant [`prɛgnənt]

▶ (形容詞) 懷孕的

例 My wife is pregnant with our second child.
我的老婆懷了第二個小孩。

●6. marry [`mærɪ]

▶ (動詞) 結婚 【三態：marry/married/married】
get married為get+pp，有「變成…狀態」之意。

●7. single [`sɪŋg!]

▶ (形容詞) 單身的

例 Are you single or married?
你單身還是已婚？

●8. lonely [`lonlɪ]

▶ (形容詞) 孤獨的，寂寞的

例 When her husband died, she was very lonely.
先生死後她非常孤獨。

▶▶▶▶▶ **4.** 健康
(health)

相關用語

1. You sound tired. Is everything OK?
   你聽起來很累,一切可好?

2. I don't feel good.
   我覺得不太舒服。

3. I have a stomachache and a headache.
   我胃疼,頭也疼。

4. Do you have a fever?
   你發燒嗎?

5. It might be the flu.
   可能是得了流感。

6. Try to get some rest.
   試著休息一下。

7. Be sure to drink lots of water.
   一定要多喝水阿。

單字、片語、句型解說

●1. sound [saʊnd]

▶ (動詞) 聽起來【+形容詞】

例 The idea sounds good.
這主意聽起來很好。

●2. tired [taɪrd]

▶ (形容詞) 疲倦的

例 You look tired today.
你今天看起來很累。

●3. stomachache [ˋstʌmək͵ek]

▶ (名詞) 胃痛

例 I got a stomachache last night.
我昨晚胃痛。

●4. headache [ˋhɛd͵ek]

▶ (名詞) 頭痛

例 My headache is gone.
我的頭痛消失了。

●5. fever [ˋfivɚ]

▶ (名詞) 發燒

例 Your child may have a high fever.
你的小孩可能發高燒了。

❸ 朋友場合

●6. flu [flu]

▶ (名詞) (口語) 流行性感冒

例 People with the flu may have a high fever.
得到流行性感冒的人也許會發高燒。

●7. be sure to +V

▶ 【務必要…，一定要…】

> sure [ʃʊr]
> (形容詞) 一定的，確信的

例 Be sure to write to me.
一定要給我寫信阿。

例 I am sure to go to the party.
我一定會去參加派對的。

Lesson6

聊寵物
(Talking About Pets)

　　寵物是人類的好朋友,台灣因少子化的現象,選擇養寵物的人也越來越多。可以說寵物已成為現代人重要的「伴侶」,台灣現在以貓、狗為大家最愛的寵物。

　　在公園裡常常可見很多愛狗人士在溜狗,或是偶爾在餐飲店裡,也會看見手上抱著愛貓、一邊享受著飲料美食、一邊閒聊的養貓族。通常養寵物的人如果聚在一起,一定會有很多狗經、貓經可以聊。

引言的關鍵單字或片語:

1. pet [pɛt]　　　　　　　(名詞)寵物

2. the trend toward fewer children
   [ðə] [trɛnd] [təˋwɔrd] [ˋfjuɚ] [ˋtʃɪldrən]
   (名詞片語)少子化

3. keep [kip]　　　　　　(動詞)飼養

4. companion [kəmˋpænjən]
   　　　　　　　　　(名詞)同伴,伴侶

5. walk [wɔk]　　　　　(動詞)蹓(狗等)

6. chat [tʃæt]　　　　　(動詞)聊天

3 朋友場合

1. 狗
(dogs)

相關用語

1. I have many dog stories to tell.
   我有很多狗經可以說。

2. My dog likes to kiss me on the face.
   我的狗喜歡吻我的臉。

3. My dogs like rolling on the grass.
   我的狗兒們喜歡在草地上打滾。

4. Do you know how to brush dogs' teeth?
   你知道如何替狗刷牙嗎？

5. Will your dog bite people?
   你的狗會咬人嗎？

6. How often do you bathe your dog?
   你多久替你的狗洗澡一次？

7. How do you train your dogs to stop barking?
   你是怎麼訓練你的狗停止吠叫的？

單字、片語、句型解說

1. story [`storɪ]

▶ (名詞) 故事

2. face [fes]

▶ (名詞) 臉

3. roll [rol]

▶ (動詞) 滾動 【三態：roll/rolled/rolled】

例 The ball rolled under the table.
球滾到桌子底下去了。

4. grass [græs]

▶ (名詞) 草，草地

5. brush [brʌʃ]

▶ (動詞) 刷，刷牙

【三態：brush/brushed/brushed】

例 Brush your teeth before going to bed.
上床前你要刷牙。

6. teeth [tiθ]

▶ (名詞) 牙齒 【tooth [tuθ]的複數】

7. bite [baɪt]

▶ (動詞) 咬，叮 【三態：bite/bit/bitten】

例 A dog bit him yesterday.
有隻狗昨天咬了他。

● 8. how often… [haʊ] [`ɔfən]

▶ 【多久…一次】

例 How often do you exercise?
你多久運動一次？

● 9. bathe [beð]

▶ (動詞) 給…洗澡

【三態：bathe/bathed/bathed】

例 I don't know how to bathe the baby.
我不知道怎麼幫嬰兒洗澡。

● 10. train [tren]

▶ (動詞) 訓練 【三態：train/trained/trained】

例 I will train you to become a good basketball player.
我會把你訓練成一個好的籃球員。

● 11. stop [stɑp]+V-ing

▶ 【停止某個正在進行的動作】

例 Stop shouting at me!
不要對我吼叫了！

● 12. bark [bɑrk]

▶ (動詞) 吠叫 【三態：bark/barked/barked】

例 Your dog is barking.
你的狗正在吠叫。

2. 貓 (cats)

相關用語

1. Do you have a cat?
   你有養貓嗎？

2. What do you use to wash your cat?
   你用什麼幫你的貓洗澡？

3. If I have asthma, should I keep a cat?
   如果我有氣喘，我應該養貓嗎？

4. My cat is afraid of strangers.
   我的貓怕陌生人。

5. My cat hates company.
   我的貓不喜歡陪伴。

6. How can I increase my cat's appetite?
   我要如何增進我的貓的食慾？

7. What do you feed your cat?
   你餵你的貓吃什麼？

🎵 **115**

單字、片語、句型解說

●1. use [juz]

▸ (動詞) 使用 【三態：use/used/used】

例 You may use my cup.
你可以用我的杯子。

●2. wash [wɑʃ]

▸ (動詞) 洗 【三態：wash/washed/washed】

例 Wash your hands before eating.
吃飯前你要先洗手。

●3. asthma [`æzmə]

▸ (名詞) 氣喘

●4. keep [kip]

▸ (動詞) 飼養 【三態：keep/kept/kept】

例 I can't keep a dog.
我不能養狗。

●5. be afraid of [bi] [ə`fred] [ɑv]+名詞／動名詞

▸ 【害怕…】

例 Are you afraid of dogs?
你怕狗嗎？

●6. stranger [ˋstrendʒɚ]

▶ (名詞) 陌生人

例 He is a stranger to me.
他對我來說是個陌生人。

●7. hate [het]

▶ (動詞) 恨，不喜歡【三態：hate/hated/hated】

例 I hate to say goodbye.
我不喜歡說再見。

●8. company [ˋkʌmpənɪ]

▶ (名詞) 陪伴

●9. increase [ɪnˋkris]

▶ (動詞) 增加

【三態：increase/increased/increased】

例 Reading can increase my knowledge.
閱讀可以增加我的知識。

●10. appetite [ˋæpə͵taɪt]

▶ (名詞) 食慾，胃口

例 He doesn't have any appetite.
他一點胃口也沒有。

●11. feed [fid]

▶ (動詞) 餵 【三態：feed/fed/fed】

例 Did you feed the baby?
你餵過小嬰兒了嗎？

MP3 116

Lesson 7

聊算命
(Talking About Fortunetelling)

　　許多人多少都有過算命的經驗，不論是從星座、血型下去分析，或是從紫微、八字的角度試著去瞭解自己的人生命運，都可說是一種有趣、奇特的經驗，也是想從中獲取人生的一些方向。

　　當然對有些人來說，算命只是為了好奇或是好玩，甚至有些人還會覺得是迷信，聽聽就算了，不用太認真。但仍是有許多人相信算命是有科學根據的，是一門非常高深的學問，其深奧及神奇之處，不能一言以蔽之。

引言的關鍵單字或片語：

1. fortunetelling [`fɔrtʃənˌtɛlɪŋ]
(名詞)算命

2. star signs [stɑr] [saɪnz] (名詞片語)星座

3. blood types [blʌd] [taɪps]
(名詞片語)血型

4. Zi Wei Dou Shu (名詞片語)紫微斗數

5. the Eight Characters [ðə] [et] [`kærɪktəz]
(名詞片語)八字

6. fate [fet]　　　　　　　(名詞)命運

7. destiny [`dɛstənɪ]　　　(名詞)命運

8. superstition [ˌsupɚ`stɪʃən]
　　　　　　　　　　(名詞)迷信

9. science [`saɪəns]　　　(名詞)科學

10. scholarship [`skɑlɚˌʃɪp]
　　　　　　　　　　(名詞)學問

❶ 工作場合

❷ 學習場合

❸ 朋友場合

1. 星座、血型
(star signs & blood types)

相關用語

1. Star signs and blood types can help to understand one's personality.
   星座跟血型有助於瞭解一個人的個性。

2. I am blood type O.
   我是O型人。

3. AB blood type people are very sensitive.
   AB型的人很敏感。

4. What's your star sign?
   你是什麼星座的？

5. My star sign is Aquarius.
   我是水瓶座的。

6. Virgos people are generally practical and hard-working.
   處女座的人通常實際又勤奮。

單字、片語、句型解說

●1. star signs [stɑr] [saɪnz]

▶ (名詞片語) 星座

例 Are you interested in star signs?
你對星座有興趣嗎？

●2. blood types [blʌd] [taɪps]

▶ (名詞片語) 血型

例 What is her blood type?
她是什麼血型？

●3. understand [ˌʌndɚˋstænd]

▶ (動詞) 了解，懂

【三態：understand/understood/understood】

例 Do you understand English?
你懂英文嗎？

●4. personality [ˌpɝsənˋælətɪ]

▶ (名詞) 人格，個性

例 She has a weak personality.
她性格軟弱。

●5. sensitive [ˋsɛnsətɪv]

▶ (形容詞) 敏感的

例 She is sensitive about her weight.
一提起她的體重，她就生氣。

●6. Aquarius [əˋkwɛrɪəs]

▶ (名詞) 水瓶座

例 Aquariuses people are liberal and open-minded.
水瓶座的人愛自由、心胸開闊。

●7. Virgo [ˋvɝgo]

▶ (名詞) 處女座

例 Virgos are born between August 23 and September 22.
處女座的人出生於八月二十三日跟九月二十二日之間。

●8. generally [ˋdʒɛnərəlɪ]

▶ (副詞) 通常

例 He generally goes to school by bus.
他通常搭公車上學。

●9. practical [ˋpræktɪk!]

▶ (形容詞) (講究) 實際的

例 Your idea is very practical.
你的想法很實際。

●10. hard-working [ˌhardˋwɝkɪŋ]

▶ (形容詞) 努力工作的，勤奮的 (=diligent)

十二星座

中文及日期	對應之英文	英文音標
魔羯座 12/22～01/19	Capricorn	[`kæprɪkɔrn]
水瓶座 01/20～02/18	Aquarius	[ə`kwɛrɪəs]
雙魚座 02/19～03/20	Pisces	[`pɪsiz]
牡羊座 03/21～04/19	Aries	[`ɛriz]
金牛座 04/20～05/20	Taurus	[`tɔrəs]
雙子座 05/21～06/21	Gemini	[`dʒɛmə͵naɪ]
巨蟹座 06/22～07/22	Cancer	[`kænsɚ]
獅子座 07/23～08/22	Leo	[`lio]
處女座 08/23～09/22	Virgo	[`vɝgo]
天秤座 09/23～10/23	Libra	[`laɪbrə]
天蠍座 10/24～11/22	Scorpio	[`skɔrpɪ͵o]
射手座 11/23～12/21	Sagittarius	[͵sædʒɪ`tɛrɪəs]

MP3 119

▶▶▶▶▶ **2.** 紫微斗數、八字
(Zi Wei Dou Shu & the Eight Characters)

相關用語

1. I had my fortune told last night.
   我昨晚去算命。

2. Do you believe in fortune-telling?
   你相信算命嗎？

3. You can get your fortune told on-line for free.
   你可以在網路上進行免費的算命。

4. By analyzing the Eight Characters, the fortuneteller told my fate.
   透過分析八字，算命師預測了我的命運。

5. This fortuneteller's predictions cover career, wealth, health and relationships.
   這個算命師的預測涵蓋了生涯、財富、健康跟關係。

6. Zi Wei Dou Shu is a calculation
   system to obtain a birth chart.
   紫微斗數是獲得命盤的運算系統。

單字、片語、句型解說

● 1. had my fortune told 是「had+O+
   pp」，表「讓⋯被⋯」。

▶ fortune [`fɔrtʃən]

(名詞) 命運

tell/told/told
(動詞) 告訴，顯示

● 2. believe in [bɪ`liv] [ɪn]+名詞/動名詞

▶【相信⋯的效用】

例 Do you believe in exercise?
   你覺得運動有用嗎？

● 3. fortune-telling [`fɔrtʃənˌtɛlɪŋ]

▶ (名詞) 算命

fortuneteller [`fɔrtʃənˌtɛlɚ]
(名詞) 算命師

● 4. get your fortune told 是「get+O+
   pp」，表「讓⋯被⋯」。

▶ tell/told/told
   (動詞) 告訴，顯示

MP3 120

●5. on-line [`ɑnˌlaɪn]

➤ (副詞) 連線地，線上地

例 I often look for information on-line.
我常常在網路上找資料。

●6. for free [fɔr] [fri]

➤ (介係詞片語) 免費

例 She got the book for free.
她免費得到這本書。

●7. by analyzing 是「by+V-ing」表「藉由…之意」。

analyze [`æn!ˌaɪz]
(動詞) 分析

【三態：analyze/analyzed/analyzed】

●8. the Eight Characters [ðə] [et] [`kærɪktəz]

➤ (名詞片語) 八字

Zi Wei Dou Shu
(名詞片語) 紫微斗數

●9. fate [fet]

➤ (名詞) 命運

例 It's our fate to meet each other.
我們能遇見彼此是命運的安排。

● 10. prediction [prɪ`dɪkʃən]

▶ (名詞) 預言，預報

例 The fortuneteller's predictions came true.
這個算命師的預言成真了。

● 11. cover [`kʌvɚ]

▶ (動詞) 包含，覆蓋

【三態：cover/covered/covered】

例 This book covers a lot of ideas.
這本書提到很多想法。

● 12. career [kə`rɪr]

▶ (名詞) 生涯

例 I am interested in the careers of great men.
我對偉人的生平感興趣。

● 13. wealth [wɛlθ]

▶ (名詞) 財富

例 He is a man of great wealth.
他是一個有錢人。

● 14. health [hɛlθ]

▶ (名詞) 健康 (狀況)

例 I am in good health.
我身體很好。

●15. relationship [rɪ`leʃən`ʃɪp]

▶ (名詞) 關係

例 I am ready for a new relationship now.
現在我已準備好要進入新的戀愛關係。

●16. calculation [ˌkælkjə`leʃən]

▶ (名詞) 計算，預測

例 By my calculation, you will pass the exam.
我估計你會通過考試。

●17. system [`sɪstəm]

▶ (名詞) 系統

例 My company needs a new computer system.
我的公司需要新的電腦系統。

●18. a birth chart [ə] [bɝθ] [tʃɑrt]

▶ (名詞片語) 命盤

例 Your birth chart may show your fate.
你的命盤也許顯示了你的命運。

Lesson 8

聊時尚
(Talking About Fashions)

愛美是人的天性。現今這個年代,不只女人愛美,男人愛美的也比比皆是。愛美不但帶來自信,為了愛美,你可能也會更注重健康和保養。

除了身體上的健康和保養,美也需要外在的裝飾,所以朋友之間的話題,也少不了時尚流行的資訊交流,彼此討論對美的追求及心得。

引言的關鍵單字或片語:

1. beauty [`bjutɪ] (名詞)美

2. confidence [`kɑnfədəns] (名詞)自信

3. health [hɛlθ] (名詞)健康

4. keep the skin in good condition [kip] [ðə] [skɪn] [ɪn] [gʊd] [kən`dɪʃən] (動詞片語)保養皮膚

5. appearance [ə`pɪrəns] (名詞)外表

6. accessory [æk`sɛsərɪ] (名詞)配件,飾品

1. 服飾、裝飾品 (clothing and accessories)

相關用語

1. In the Ximending district, boutiques attract many young people.

   西門町的精品店吸引了很多年輕人。

2. I love to try on trendy women's clothing.

   我喜歡試穿流行的女性服飾。

3. Where can I find cheap clothes and accessories?

   我可以在哪裡找到便宜的衣服跟飾品？

4. Where do you buy necklaces, earrings, bracelets, rings and hair accessories?

   你在哪裡買項鍊、耳環、手鐲、戒指跟髮飾品？

5. Every item in this store is affordable and is of good quality.

   這家店的東西價格合理而且品質很好。

單字、片語、句型解說

● 1. boutique [bu`tik]

▶ (名詞) 精品店

例 This boutique sells nice accessories.
這家精品店的飾品很不錯。

● 2. try on [traɪ] [ɑn]

▶ (動詞片語) 試穿

例 I'd like to try on the jacket.
我想要試穿夾克。

● 3. trendy [`trɛndɪ]

▶ (形容詞) 時髦的，流行的

例 Are you a trendy person?
你是一個時髦的人嗎？

● 4. clothing [`kloðɪŋ]

▶ (名詞) (總稱) 衣服，衣著

clothes [kloz]
(名詞) 衣服

● 5. accessory [æk`sɛsərɪ]

▶ (名詞) 配件，飾品

例 You may need some hair accessories.
你也許需要一些髮飾品。

●6. necklace [`nɛklɪs]

▶ (名詞) 項鍊

> earring [`ɪr/rɪŋ]
> (名詞) 耳環

> bracelet [`breslɪt]
> (名詞) 手鐲

> ring [rɪŋ]
> (名詞) 戒指

●7. item [`aɪtəm]

▶ (名詞) 項目，品目

例 She needs to buy some baby items.
她需要買一些嬰兒用品。

●8. affordable [ə`fɔrdəb!]

▶ (形容詞) 負擔得起的

例 Is the car affordable for you?
這車子你負擔得起嗎？

●9. quality [`kwɑlətɪ]

▶ (名詞) 品質

例 The jacket is of good quality.
這件夾克品質很好。

2. 外型打扮、保養
(dressing up & carrying age)

相關用語

1. You carry your age well.
   你駐顏有術。

2. Would you share your skin care tips for cleansing and moisturizing?
   你願意跟我分享皮膚清潔跟保濕的祕訣嗎？

3. I think you should consult a dermatologist about your skin.
   我覺得你應該去給皮膚科醫生看皮膚。

4. This skin product may improve the quality of your skin.
   這個保養品也許可以改善你的膚質。

5. You look neat and stylish today.
   你今天的樣子很好又時髦。

6. The color of the shirt matches that of the trousers well.
   襯衫的顏色跟褲子很相配。

單字、片語、句型解說

●1. carry [ˋkærɪ]

▶ (動詞) 隱瞞，不顯出 (年老等)

【三態：carry/carried/carried】

age [edʒ]
(名詞) 年齡

●2. skin care [skɪn] [kɛr]

▶ (名詞片語) 皮膚保養

skin [skɪn]
(名詞) 皮膚

care [kɛr]
(名詞) 照顧

●3. tip [tɪp]

▶ (名詞) 訣竅

例 What are your tips for learning English?
你學英文的訣竅是什麼？

●4. cleanse [klɛnz]

▶ (動詞) 清潔，清洗

【三態：cleanse/cleansed/cleansed】

例 What do you use to cleanse your face?
你用什麼洗臉？

●5. moisturize [ˋmɔɪstʃəˌraɪz]

► (動詞) 使濕潤

【三態：moisturize/moisturized/moisturized】

例 What do you use to moisturize your hair?
你用什麼潤髮？

●6. consult [kənˋsʌlt]

► (動詞) 請教，看醫生

【三態：consult/consulted/consulted】

例 You need to consult a doctor.
你需要看醫生。

●7. dermatologist [ˌdɝməˋtɑlədʒɪst]

► (名詞) 皮膚科醫生

例 She is a famous dermatologist.
她是一個有名的皮膚科醫生。

●8. neat [nit]

► (形容詞) 整齊的，樣子好的

例 You look neat in the picture.
照片裡的你看起來樣子很好。

9. stylish [`staɪlɪʃ]

▶ (形容詞) 時髦的，流行的

例 Your hair is stylish.
你的髮型很時髦。

MP3 126

10. match [mætʃ]

▶ (動詞) 和…相配

【三態：match/matched/matched】

例 Your shirt doesn't match your shoes.
你的襯衫跟你的鞋子不搭。

11. 此句中 that of the trousers 的 that = the color。

▶ that用來代替前面提過的單數名詞

trousers [`traʊzɚz]
(名詞)褲子

12.【補充】常見的衣物：

▶ (1)jacket (夾克)

(2)skirt (裙子)

(3)sweater (毛衣)

(4)shirt (襯衫)

(5)hat (帽子)

(6)shoe (鞋子)

Lesson9
聊交通工具
(Transport)

　　不論和外國朋友從事什麼活動，出門在外一定需要交通工具代步，尤其在台北，因為停車不易，抑或是為了節省費用，也因為節能減碳環保觀念的推廣，很多民眾出門時寧可選擇搭乘捷運或公車。

　　不過有時候因為活動及人數的需求及方便性的考量，自行開車或是騎機車也是常見的方式。尤其在一些歐美國家，騎機車可能沒有那麼普遍，更是外國人可能會感到好奇的話題。

引言的關鍵單字或片語：

1. transport [`træns͵pɔrt] (名詞)交通工具

2. parking [`pɑrkɪŋ] (名詞)停車

3. environmental protection [ɪn͵vaɪrən`mɛnt!]
   [prə`tɛkʃən] (名詞片語)環保

4. MRT(= Mass Rapid Transit)
   大眾捷運系統

5. bus [bʌs] (名詞)公車

6. motorcycle [`motə͵saɪk!]
   (名詞)摩托車，機車

① 工作場合

② 單畜場合

③ 朋友場合

1. 大眾運輸工具 (public transportation)

相關用語

1. Will you take the MRT or the bus?
   你要搭捷運還是公車？

2. It's convenient to use an EasyCard to take the MRT and the bus.
   用悠遊卡搭捷運和公車很方便。

3. It's very comfortable to ride in the clean and air-conditioned MRT cars.
   搭乘乾淨又有空調的捷運車廂是非常舒適的。

4. Many people in Taipei now take the MRT to go to work or go to school.
   現在台北有很多人搭乘捷運上班或上學。

5. If you take the bus in Taipei, it will only cost you about NT$15 to 30.
   如果你在台北搭公車，大約只要花費台幣十五到三十元。

單字、片語、句型解說

●1. take [tek]

▸ (動詞) 搭乘 【三態：take/took/taken】

例 Can you take a bus to the station?
你可以搭公車去車站嗎？

●2. MRT (= Mass Rapid Transit)

▸ 大眾捷運系統

> EasyCard [ˋizɪ ˌkɑrd]
> (名詞)悠遊卡

●3. comfortable [ˋkʌmfəˌtəb!]

▸ (形容詞) 舒服的

例 Do you feel comfortable in the air-conditioned room?
你在冷氣房裡覺得舒服嗎？

●4. ride [raɪd]

▸ (動詞) 乘坐 【三態：ride/rode/ridden】

例 Do you have a ticket to ride in the train cars?
你有票可以搭火車嗎？

MP3 129

●5. clean [klin]

► (形容詞) 乾淨的

例 Your room is very clean.
你的房間好乾淨。

●6. air-conditioned [`ɛrkənˌdɪʃənd]

► (形容詞) 有空調的

例 Is your room air-conditioned?
你的房間有冷氣嗎？

●7. car [kɑr]

► (名詞) 車廂

例 How many cars are there in the train?
這列火車有多少車廂？

●8. 事或物+cost [kɔst]+人+錢

► 【某事或某物花費…人多少錢】
cost三態同形

例 This book cost him 20 US dollars.
這本書花了他美金二十元。

2. 汽機車
(cars & motorcycles)

相關用語

1. How long have you been driving?
   你開車多久了？

2. You need an international driver's license to drive a car in Taiwan.
   要在台灣開車的話，你需要國際駕照。

3. Do you know how to rent a car in Taipei?
   你知道如何在台北租車嗎？

4. Will you drive me to the company?
   你會開車載我到公司嗎？

5. Parking is not easy in Taipei.
   在台北停車不容易。

6. It may be dangerous to ride a motorcycle in Taipei.
   在台北騎摩托車也許是危險的。

7. You have to wear a helmet while riding a motorcycle in Taiwan.
   在台灣騎機車需要戴安全帽。

❶ 工作場合
❷ 學習場合
❸ 朋友場合

MP3 130

單字、片語、句型解說

● 1. how long [haʊ] [lɔn]…

▶【…多久了？】

例 How long have you been waiting?
你等多久了？

● 2. have been driving 為 have been+
V-ing

▶ 為「現在完成進行式」，表從過去持續到現
在的動作或狀態。

例 It has been raining for three days.
已經下了三天的雨了。(雨到現在還沒有停)

● 3. international [ˌɪntɚˈnæʃnḷ]

▶ (形容詞) 國際的

例 I will go to an international meeting
next week.
下週我將參加一個國際性的會議。

● 4. a driver's license [ə] [ˈdraɪvɚz]
[ˈlaɪsəns]

▶ (名詞片語) 駕照

例 Do you have a driver's license?
你有駕照嗎？

●5. rent [rɛnt]

▶ (動詞) 租用 【三態：rent/rented/rented】

例 I need to rent an apartment in Taipei.
我需要在台北租一間公寓。

●6. parking [`pɑrkɪŋ]

▶ (名詞) 停車

例 No parking here!
這裡禁止停車！

●7. dangerous [`dendʒərəs]

▶ (形容詞) 危險的

例 It is dangerous to drive in the rain.
雨中開車是危險的。

●8. ride [raɪd]

▶ (動詞) 騎…

【三態：ride/rode/ridden】

例 I often ride a bicycle to work.
我常常騎腳踏車上班。

●9. have to+V

▶ 【必須…】

例 He has to get up early every day.
他必須每天早起。

● 10. wear [wɛr]

► (動詞) 穿⋯，戴⋯

【三態：wear/wore/worn】

例 I have to wear glasses while reading.
我在讀東西時必須戴眼鏡。　　**MP3 131**

● 11. helmet [ˋhɛlmɪt]

► (名詞) 安全帽

例 Is it hot to wear a helmet?
戴安全帽會很熱嗎？

● 12. 此句中的 while riding=while you are riding

► while [hwaɪl]

(副詞連接詞)

正當⋯【所接的句子常用「進行式」】

例 The phone rang while I was listening to music.
當我正在聽音樂時，電話響了起來。

例 Mary was almost hit by a car while she was crossing the street.
瑪莉過馬路的時候差點被車子撞到。

【補充】while 也有「然而」的意思。

例 Julia likes tea while Lisa likes coffee.
茱麗葉喜歡茶，而麗莎喜歡咖啡。

Lesson 11
聊購物
(Going Shopping)

　　在台灣購物可說是非常方便，光是便利商店、超級市場，走在街頭，隨意抬頭一望，可能在百步之內就可看到。台灣便利商店之多，在外國人的眼中，可說是一種寶島奇景了。除了便利商店、超級市場，如果想要買到更多樣化、或是更精緻的食材或日用品，那就可以去像太平洋百貨公司或是新光三越等等這樣的購物中心，通常這些地方因為空間廣大，加上多數結合了提供現場飲食的餐館，因此也是不少人休閒放鬆的一種方式。而跟大多數一般家庭日常生活最緊密相關的，也許就是傳統市場，尤其是對三餐自己開伙的家庭而言，傳統市場絕對是買到新鮮、道地食材的好地方。

引言的關鍵單字或片語：

1. go shopping [go] [ˋʃɑpɪŋ]
(動詞片語)去購物

2. a convenience store [ə] [kənˋvinjəns] [stor]
(名詞片語)便利商店

3. supermarket [`supɚˏmɑrkɪt]
(名詞)超級市場

4. a department store [ə] [dɪ`pɑrtmənt] [stor]
(名詞片語)百貨公司

5. a shopping mall [ə] [`ʃɑpɪŋ] [mɔl]
(名詞片語)購物中心(同義片語為 a shopping
center)

6. a traditional market [ə] [trə`dɪʃən!]
[`mɑrkɪt]
(名詞片語)傳統市場

▶▶▶▶ *1.* 便利商店、超級市場 (convenience stores & supermarkets)

相關用語

1. There are two convenience stores around here.
   這附近有兩家便利商店。

2. The convenience store is open 24 hours a day.
   這家便利商店二十四小時營業。

3. You can use the ATM at the convenience store.
   你可以使用便利商店裡面的自動提款機。

4. Taiwan's three leading convenience store chains are 7-Eleven, Family Mart, and Hi Life.
   台灣的三大便利商店連鎖店是統一超商 7-11、全家跟萊爾富。

① 工作場合
② 學習場合
③ 朋友場合

5. He's going to the supermarket. Do you want to go with him?

他要去超市，你想跟他一起去嗎？

6. I often buy groceries in Carrefour.

我常常在家樂福買食品雜貨。

7. I can take you to visit Taiwan's supermarkets, such as Carrefour, A-mart, Wellcome, RT Mart, PX Mart and Costco.

我可以帶你參觀台灣的超級市場，比如說家樂福、愛買、頂好、大潤發、全聯跟好市多。

8. There is a supermarket in this department store.

這家百貨公司有一間超級市場。

9. You can get cash and pay bills in 7-11 stores.

你可以在7-11超商領取現金跟付帳單。

134

單字、片語、句型解說

●1. a convenience store [ə] [kən`vinjəns] [stor]

▶ (名詞片語) 便利商店

例 There are two convenience stores in the vicinity.
附近有兩家便利商店。

●2. open [`opən]

▶ (形容詞) 營業的

例 This store is open from 10:00 a.m. to 8:00 p.m..
這家店從早上十點營業到晚上八點。

●3. ATM (= Automatic Teller Machine)

▶ 自動提款機

例 I often use the bank's ATM to get cash.
我常用銀行的提款機領取現金。

●4. leading [`lidɪŋ]

▶ (形容詞) 領導的，帶頭的

例 He works in a leading computer company.
他在一家電腦龍頭公司工作。

● 5. chain [tʃen]

▶ (名詞) 連鎖店

例 You can buy the new product in the chain stores.
你可以在連鎖店買到這個新產品。

● 6. 7-Eleven [`sɛvən] [ɪ`lɛvən]

▶ 統一超商 7-11

Family Mart [`fæməlɪ] [mɑrt]
全家

Hi Life [haɪ] [laɪf]
萊爾富

● 7. supermarket [`supɚ͵mɑrkɪt]

▶ (名詞) 超級市場

例 My mother usually goes to the super-market after work.
我媽媽通常在下班後去超級市場。

● 8. grocery [`grosərɪ]

▶ (名詞) 食品雜貨，南北貨

例 Do you need to buy a lot of groceries?
你需要買很多雜貨嗎？

135

•9. Carrefour [`kærə‚fʊr]

▶ 家樂福

> A-mart [`e‚mɑrt]
> 愛買

> Wellcome [`wɛlkəm]
> 頂好

> RT Mart [ɑr] [ti] [mɑrt]
> 大潤發

> PX Mart [pi] [ɛks] [mɑrt]
> 全聯

> Costco [`kɔst‚ko]
> 好市多

•10. take+人+to+V

▶ 【帶…人去…】

例 I will take you to visit my school.
我會帶你參觀我的學校。
【補充】人+**take**+時間+**to V**
【…人花時間去...】

例 I take some time to practice piano
every day.
我每天花一點時間練鋼琴。

▶▶▶▶ 2. 傳統市場、購物中心
(traditional markets & shopping malls)

相關用語

1. Would you like to go to the traditional market with me?
   你要跟我一起去傳統市場嗎？

2. What are you shopping for?
   你要買什麼？

3. The traditional market sells very good meat and vegetables.
   這個傳統市場賣的肉及蔬菜很不錯。

4. You can even buy clothes and shoes in this traditional market.
   你甚至可以在這個傳統市場裡買衣服和鞋子。

5. Beverages are on sale in the shopping mall.
   購物中心的飲料在特價。

單字、片語、句型解說

● **1. a traditional market** [ə] [trə`dɪʃən!] [`mɑrkɪt]

▶ (名詞片語) 傳統市場

> traditional [trə`dɪʃən!]
> (形容詞) 傳統的

> market [`mɑrkɪt]
> (名詞) 市場

例 My mother goes to a nearby traditional market every day.
我媽媽每天去鄰近的傳統市場。

● **2. meat** [mit]

▶ (名詞) 肉

> vegetable [`vɛdʒətəb!]
> (名詞) 蔬菜

例 Do you like to eat meat or vegetables?
你喜歡吃肉還是蔬菜？

● **3. clothes** [kloz]

▶ (名詞) 衣服

> shoe [ʃu]
> (名詞) 鞋子

例 Put on your clothes and shoes quickly.

快點把你的衣服跟鞋子穿好。

●4. on sale [ɑn] [sel]

▶ (介係詞片語) 特價中

例 These computers are on sale.

這些電腦在特價中。

●5. a shopping mall [ə] [`ʃɑpɪŋ] [mɔl]

▶ (名詞片語) 購物中心

(同義片語為a shopping center [ə] [`ʃɑpɪŋ] [`sɛntɚ])

shopping [`ʃɑpɪŋ]
(形容詞)購物的

mall [mɔl]
(名詞)大規模購物中心

center [`sɛntɚ]
(名詞)中心

例 There is a shopping mall near the park.

公園附近有一間購物中心。

Lesson11
聊常見的機構
(Talking About Common Institutions)

　　日常生活中大家一定免不了偶爾要去類似銀行或是郵局這樣常見的機構處理一些事情，在台灣生活的外國朋友也不例外。

　　其它常見的機構諸如圖書館、文化中心等等，也是介紹外國友人可以常去的好地方，尤其對喜愛閱讀、文化活動的外國友人而言，這樣的資訊分享一定可以豐富其生活與心靈。

引言的關鍵單字或片語：

1. common [ˋkɑmən]　　　(形容詞)常見的

2. institution [ˌɪnstəˋtjuʃən] (名詞)機構

3. bank [bæŋk]　　　　　(名詞)銀行

4. a post office [ə] [post] [ˋɔfɪs]
　　　　　　　　　　(名詞片語)郵局

5. library [ˋlaɪˌbrɛrɪ]　　(名詞)圖書館

6. a cultural center [ə] [ˋkʌltʃərəl] [ˋsɛntɚ]
　　　　　　　　　　(名詞片語)文化中心

① 工作場合

② 學習場合

③ 朋友場合

1. 銀行、郵局 (banks & post offices)

相關用語

1. I need to go to the bank to pay my credit card bills.
   我需要去銀行付我信用卡的帳單。

2. Going to a bank is a common errand for me.
   去銀行辦事是我經常做的事。

3. I deposited a check into my account this morning.
   今天早上我在帳戶裡存了一張支票。

4. Banks and post offices are always crowded at lunchtime.
   銀行跟郵局在午餐時間總是擠滿了人。

5. I often go to the post office to mail some things at lunchtime.
   我常在中午用餐時間去郵局寄一些東西。

6. You can buy stamps at the post office.
   你可以在郵局買郵票。

單字、片語、句型解說

●1. pay [pe]

▶ (動詞) 付錢 【三態：pay/paid/paid】

例 How much do I have to pay?
我需要付多少錢？

●2. a credit card [ə] [ˋkrɛdɪt] [kɑrd]

▶ (名詞片語) 信用卡

例 You can pay by credit card.
你可以用信用卡付錢。

●3. bill [bɪl]

▶ (名詞) 帳單

例 How much is the gas bill?
瓦斯費多少錢？

●4. common [ˋkɑmən]

▶ (形容詞) 普通的，常見的

例 It is common for people to exercise in a park.
公園裡常見有民眾在運動。

●5. errand [ˋɛrənd]

▶ (名詞) 差事

例 Do you have time to run errands for me?

你有時間為我跑腿嗎？

●6. deposit [dɪˋpɑzɪt]

▶ (動詞) 寄存

【三態：deposit/deposited/deposited】

例 I deposited 6,000 dollars in the bank yesterday.

昨天我在銀行存了六千元。

●7. check [tʃɛk]

▶ (名詞) 支票

例 Can you write me a check?

你可以開一張支票給我嗎？

●8. account [əˋkaʊnt]

▶ (名詞) 帳戶

例 What's your account number?

你的帳號是多少？

●9. crowded [ˋkraʊdɪd]

▶ (形容詞) 擁擠的

例 The bus is very crowded.
公車上擠滿了人。

● 10. mail [mel]

▶ (動詞) 郵寄 【三態：mail/mailed/mailed】

例 Did you mail the letter yesterday?
你昨天把信寄出去了嗎？

● 11. lunchtime [ˈlʌntʃˌtaɪm]

▶ (名詞) 午餐時間

例 How long is your lunchtime?
你的午餐時間有多久？

● 12. stamp [stæmp]

▶ (名詞) 郵票

例 He likes to collect stamps.
他喜歡集郵。

● 13.【補充】銀行、郵局常見用語：

▶ (1)open an account (開戶)

(2)withdraw money (提款)

(3)save money (存款)

(4)remit money (匯款)

(5)transfer money (劃撥)

2. 圖書館、文化中心
(libraries & cultural centers)

相關用語

1. I often borrow books from the nearby library.

   我常常從附近的圖書館借書。

2. I have to return these books at the end of the month.

   我必須在月底歸還這些書。

3. Some libraries lend magazines and DVDs, too.

   有些圖書館也出借雜誌跟影碟。

4. Those books are due today.

   那些書今天到期。

5. There are many art and cultural activities in the Taipei Cultural Center.

   臺北市立社會教育館有很多藝文活動。

6. The National Theater and National Concert Hall are Taiwan's primary national performing arts venues.
   國家戲劇院跟國家音樂廳是台灣主要的國家級表演藝術場地。

7. You can enjoy many activities in the community cultural center.
   你可以在社區文化中心享受很多活動的樂趣。

8. Do you want to watch a free show in the community cultural center with me?
   你想要跟我一起去社區文化中心觀賞免費的表演嗎？

9. There is a free Taiwanese folk opera performance in the cultural center.
   文化中心有一場免費的歌仔戲表演。

10. Do you want to watch a Taiwanese puppet show with me in the community cultural center?
    你想跟我一起去社區文化中心看布袋戲嗎？

單字、片語、句型解說

●1. borrow [`baro]+東西+from+對象

▶ 【從…借…】

【三態:borrow/borrowed/borrowed】

例 Can I borrow some money from you?
我可以跟你借點錢嗎?

●2. nearby [`nɪr͵baɪ]

▶ (形容詞) 附近的

例 I want to go to a nearby hospital.
我要去附近的醫院。

●3. return [rɪ`tɝn]

▶ (動詞) 歸還

【三態:return/returned/returned】

例 When will you return the book to me?
你什麼時候要還我書?

●4. lend [lɛnd]+東西+to+對象

▶ 【借…給…】

【三態:lend/lent/lent】

例 Can you lend the book to me?
你可以把書借給我嗎?

●5. due [dju]

▶ (形容詞) 到期的

例 The check is due this month.
支票這個月到期。

●6. the Taipei Cultural Center

▶ [ðə] [ˋtaɪˋpe] [ˋkʌltʃərəl] [ˋsɛntɚ]

(名詞片語)臺北市立社會教育館

the National Theater [ðə] [ˋnæʃən!] [ˋθɪətɚ]

(名詞片語) 國家戲劇院

the National Concert Hall [ðə] [ˋnæʃən!]

[ˋkɑnsɚt] [hɔl]

(名詞片語) 國家音樂廳

●7. primary [ˋpraɪˏmɛrɪ]

▶ (形容詞) 主要的

例 She is our primary client.
她是我們主要的客戶。

●8. national [ˋnæʃən!]

▶ (形容詞) 國家的

例 This is a national museum.
這是一間國家博物館。

●9. performing arts

► [pɚˋfɔrmɪŋ] [ɑrts]
(名詞片語) 表演藝術

例 Miss Hsu majors in performing arts.
許小姐主修表演藝術。

●10. venue [ˋvɛnju]

► (名詞) 場地

例 This is a good venue for performing arts.
這是表演藝術的好場地。

●11. a community cultural center

► [ə] [kəˋmjunətɪ] [ˋkʌltʃərəl] [ˋsɛntɚ]
(名詞片語) 社區文化中心

例 There will be an outdoor concert at the community cultural center this Saturday.
這週六社區文化中心將有一場戶外音樂會。

●12. a Taiwanese folk opera

► [ə] [͵taɪwəˋniz] [fok] [ˋɑpərə]
(名詞片語)歌仔戲

●13. a Taiwanese puppet show

► [ə] [͵taɪwəˋniz] [ˋpʌpɪt] [ʃo]
(名詞片語)布袋戲

Lesson 12
聊國粹
(Talking About the Quintessence of Chinese Culture)

　　外國人對中國國粹大多感到興趣，諸如麻將、武術、中醫等等，可說是中國文化及智慧的累積，可帶來樂趣、可帶來健康、可增進情誼、可學習哲理，應該是很快可以和外國人聊成一片的話題。

引言的關鍵單字或片語：

1. quintessence [kwɪn`tɛsəns]

   (名詞)精華，典型

2. mahjong [mɑ`dʒɔŋ]　(名詞)麻將

3. a martial art [ə] [`mɑrʃəl] [ɑrt]

   (名詞片語)武術

4. Chinese medicine [`tʃaɪ`niz] [`mɛdəsən]
   (名詞片語)中醫

5. Chinese culture [`tʃaɪ`niz] [`kʌltʃɚ]
   (名詞片語)中國文化

6. wisdom [`wɪzdəm]　(名詞)智慧

7. pleasure [`plɛʒɚ]　(名詞)樂趣

① 工作場合

② 學習場合

③ 朋友場合

8. health [hɛlθ] (名詞)健康

9. friendly feelings [`frɛndlɪ] [`filɪŋz]
(名詞片語)情誼

10. philosophy [fə`lɑsəfɪ] (名詞)哲理

►►►► *1.* 麻將
(mahjong)

相關用語

1. Mahjong originated in China.
   麻將起源於中國。

2. Mahjong is commonly played by four players.
   麻將通常是四個人玩。

3. Mahjong is a game of strategy and calculation.
   麻將是策略及計算的遊戲。

4. Mahjong is commonly played with a set of 144 tiles.
   麻將玩的時候通常有一百四十四張牌。

5. In Taiwan, usually each player begins by receiving sixteen tiles.
   在台灣,通常每個麻將玩家一開始時抓十六張牌。

6. There are three different suits numbered 1 to 9: bamboos, characters, and circles.

有三種一到九的牌組：索子、萬子、筒子。

單字、片語、句型解說

●1. originate [əˋrɪdʒəˌnet]

▶ (動詞) 起源，來自

例 The idea originated from me.
這主意是我想出來的。

●2. commonly [ˋkɑmənlɪ]

▶ (副詞) 通常，一般

●3. is commonly played 是被動式，「be+pp=is +played」。

▶ player [ˋpleə]

(名詞) 遊戲的人，打牌的人

●4. game [gem]

▶ (名詞) 遊戲

●5. strategy [ˋstrætədʒɪ]

▶ (名詞) 策略，計謀

●6. calculation [ˌkælkjəˋleʃən]

▶ (名詞) 計算

●7. set [sɛt]

▶ (名詞) 一套，一副，一組

MP3 145

●8. tile [taɪl]

▶ (名詞) (遊戲的)牌

例 A set of Mahjong usually has at least 136 tiles.

一組麻將通常至少有一百三十六張牌。

●9. by+V-ing (receive 的 V-ing= receiving)，表「藉由…，透過…」。

▶ receive [rɪˋsiv]

(動詞) 收到，得到

●10. suit [sut]

▶ (名詞) 套，副，組

例 A deck of cards has four suits.
一副牌有四組花色。

● 11. number [`nʌmbɚ]

▶ (動詞) 編號

　　這邊是⋯(which are) numbered 1 to 9，are numbered為 be+pp (被動式)。

● 12. bamboo [bæm`bu]

▶ (名詞) 竹子，(麻將的)索子

> character [`kærɪktɚ]
> (名詞) 字，(麻將的)萬子

> circle [`sɝk!]
> (名詞) 圓，(麻將的)筒子

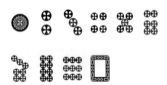

2. 武術 (martial arts)

相關用語

1. Martial arts have developed over the centuries in China.
   武術在中國已發展了好幾世紀。

2. Martial arts involve a number of fighting styles.
   武術包含多個武打風格。

3. Some training methods of martial arts are inspired by Chinese philosophies.
   武術中的一些訓練方法受到中國哲理的啟發。

4. Daoist philosophy has influenced the Chinese martial arts to a certain extent.
   道家哲理在某種程度上影響了中國武術。

5. Many people practice martial arts for self-defense.
   許多人習武是為了防身。

6. Kung fu movies came to international attention from the 1970s.

功夫電影自一九七〇年代獲得國際性的矚目。

MP3 146

單字、片語、句型解說

● 1. a martial art [ə] [ˋmɑrʃəl] [ɑrt]

▶ (名詞片語) 武術

> a martial artist [ə] [ˋmɑrʃəl] [ˋɑrtɪst]
> (名詞片語) 武術家

例 Kevin is interested in Chinese martial arts. He wants to be a martial artist.
凱文對中國武術感興趣。他想成為武術家。

● 2. develop [dɪˋvɛləp]

▶ (動詞) 發展

例 Reading develops the mind.
閱讀發展心智。

● 3. century [ˋsɛntʃʊrɪ]

▶ (名詞) 世紀，一百年

例 One century is 100 years.
一世紀是一百年。

4. a number of [ə] [ˋnʌmbɚ] [ɑv]

▶ (片語) 一些，許多

例 A number of students have left the classroom.
一些學生已經離開了教室。

5. fighting [ˋfaɪtɪŋ]

▶ (形容詞) 戰鬥的，鬥爭的

> style [staɪl]
> (名詞) 風格，種類

> a fighting style [ə] [ˋfaɪtɪŋ] [staɪl]
> (名詞片語) 武打風格

6. training [ˋtrenɪŋ]

▶ (形容詞) 訓練的

method [ˋmɛθəd]

▶ (名詞) 方法

a training method [ə] [ˋtrenɪŋ] [ˋmɛθəd]

▶ (名詞片語) 訓練方法

7. inspire [ɪnˋspaɪr]

▶ (動詞) 激勵，啟發

例 The book inspired the artist.
這本書使藝術家靈思泉湧。

●8. philosophy [fə`lɑsəfɪ]

▶ (名詞) 哲學，哲理

例 The book is full of philosophy.
這本書富含哲理。

🔊 **147**

●9. Daoist [`daʊɪst]

▶ (形容詞) 道家的

例 The book is about Daoist philosophy.
這是本有關道家哲理的書。

●10. influence [`ɪnflʊəns]

▶ (動詞) 影響

這邊的has influenced是「has+pp」，為現在完成式。

●11. to a certain extent [tu] [ə] [`sɜˈtən] [ɪk`stɛnt]

▶ (介係詞片語) 某種程度上

例 To a certain extent you are right.
某種程度上你是對的。

●12. practice [`præktɪs]

▶ (動詞) 實行，練習

例 I practice the guitar every day.
我每天練習彈吉他。

- •13. self-defense [ˌsɛlfdɪˋfɛns]
  - ▶ (名詞) 自衛
  - 例 This is a self-defense class for women.
    這是給女性的防身課。

- •14. international [ˌɪntɚˋnæʃən!]
  - ▶ (形容詞) 國際的

- •15. attention [əˋtɛnʃən]
  - ▶ (名詞) 注意，注意力

▶▶▶ **3.** 中醫
(Chinese medicine)

相關用語

1. Chinese medicine is based on the Five Phases and Yin-yang theory.
   中醫根據的是五行跟陰陽之道。

2. Chinese herbal medicine is a major aspect of Chinese medicine.
   中藥是中醫主要的部分。

3. Acupuncture relieves pain and treats various diseases.

   針灸減輕疼痛，治療各種疾病。

4. Tui na and Cupping are two types of Chinese massage.

   推拿和拔罐是兩種中國按摩術。

5. Qigōng is a Chinese medicine system of exercise and meditation.

   氣功是一種中醫的運動和禪修系統。

6. Gua Sha is often used to treat respiratory diseases.

   刮痧常被用來治療呼吸道疾病。

 148

單字、片語、句型解說

●1. Chinese medicine [`tʃaɪ`niz] [`mɛdəsən]

▶ (名詞片語) 中醫

●2. be based on+名詞/動名詞

▶ 【基於…，根據…】

例 The book is based on a true story.
   這書是根據真實故事所寫成的。

●3. the Five Phases theory

▶ [ðə] [faɪv] [ˋfezɪz] [ˋθɪərɪ]

(名詞片語) 五行理論

the Yin-yang theory [ðə] [jɪn] [jæŋ] [ˋθɪərɪ]

(名詞片語) 陰陽理論

●4. herbal [ˋhɝb!]

▶ (形容詞) 草本的

●5. Chinese herbal medicine

▶ [ˋtʃaɪˋniz] [ˋhɝb!] [ˋmɛdəsən]

(名詞片語) 中藥

例 Chinese herbal medicine has a long history.

中藥有很長的歷史。

●6. acupuncture [ˋækjʊˌpʌŋktʃɚ]

▶ (名詞) 針灸

●7. relieve [rɪˋliv]

▶ (動詞) 緩和，減輕

●8. pain [pen]

▶ (名詞) 疼痛，痛苦

例 I have a pain in my stomach.

我胃痛。

9. treat [trit]

▶ (動詞) 對待，治療

例 Dr. Huang can treat this disease.
黃醫師可以治這種病。

10. disease [dɪ`ziz]

▶ (名詞) 疾病

例 Eating fruits and vegetables can help prevent disease.
吃蔬果有益預防疾病。

11. massage [mə`sɑʒ]

▶ (名詞) 按摩

例 Can a massage relieve my back pain?
按摩可以減輕我的背痛嗎？

12. meditation [ˌmɛdə`teʃən]

▶ (名詞) 默想，禪修

13. respiratory [rɪ`spaɪrəˌtorɪ]

▶ (形容詞) 呼吸的

跟老外聊天有這本就夠了

雅致風靡 典藏文化

親愛的顧客您好，感謝您購買這本書。即日起，填寫讀者回函卡寄回至
本公司，我們每月將抽出一百名回函讀者，寄出精美禮物並享有生日當
月購書優惠！想知道更多更即時的消息，歡迎加入"永續圖書粉絲團"
您也可以選擇傳真、掃描或用本公司準備的免郵回函寄回，謝謝。

傳真電話：（02）8647-3660　　　電子信箱：yungjiuh@ms45.hinet.net

姓名：		性別：	□男　　□女
出生日期：　年　　月　　日		電話：	
學歷：		職業：	
E-mail：			
地址：□□□			
從何處購買此書：		購買金額：	元
購買本書動機：□封面 □書名 □排版 □內容 □作者 □偶然衝動			
你對本書的意見： 內容：□滿意□尚可□待改進　　編輯：□滿意□尚可□待改進 封面：□滿意□尚可□待改進　　定價：□滿意□尚可□待改進			
其他建議：			

總經銷：永續圖書有限公司

永續圖書線上購物網
www.foreverbooks.com.tw

您可以使用以下方式將回函寄回。

您的回覆，是我們進步的最大動力，謝謝。

① 使用本公司準備的免郵回函寄回。

② 傳真電話：（02）8647-3660

③ 掃描圖檔寄到電子信箱：

　　yungjiuh@ms45.hinet.net

- -

沿此線對折後寄回，謝謝。

廣　告　回　信
基隆郵局登記證
基隆廣字第056號

２２１０３

 雅典文化事業有限公司　收

新北市汐止區大同路三段194號9樓之1

雅致風靡　典藏文化